Fitting In

By Silvia Violet

Dedication

To all those who pushed me to write faster, especially Christy and Sharon, and to Erika, Hank and Mathilde for helping me along the way.

Silvia Violet

Fitting In by Silvia Violet

Copyright © 2013 by Silvia Violet

Cover art by Meredith Russell

Edited by Erika Orrick

Published in the United States of America.

Fitting In is a work of fiction. Names, places, characters, and incidents are either the product of the author's imagination or are fictionalized. Any resemblance to any actual persons, living or dead, is entirely coincidental.

The author acknowledges the trademarked status of the following wordmarks used in this story:

Coke: The Coca-Cola Company

NCAA: The National Collegiate Athletic Association

Fitting In

Star Trek: Paramount Pictures Corporation

Battlestar Galactica: Universal City Studios

Stargate: MGM Studios

Chapter One

Two cops walked into a bar. Mason, the bartender, waited for the punch line, because no way in hell were these ridiculously hot men real cops. They were one hundred percent fantasy material. He hoped to hell they were strippers, and they'd be willing to do a private performance for him.

Their dark blue uniforms were snug, hugging their bodies in all the right places. The taller of the two men was big enough to bench-press Mason. His shirt looked like it might burst at the seams, and Mason hoped it would. Dark, wavy hair fell over his forehead and softened the hard lines of his face. His eyes were dark without being warm, just right for a cop.

His partner was shorter, about Mason's own five foot eleven or so. He had buzz-cut dirty blond hair and blue eyes. He looked younger than his partner, like he hadn't been out of the academy for long, but he was just as ridiculously hot as the bigger man. His looks were the all-American-boy type. He'd probably played baseball in school and won the heart of every girl he smiled at. He was a perfect counter to his partner's rough, domineering appeal. They could play a scintillating game of good cop, bad cop, and Mason would love for them to play it with him.

If Mason were in a porno, the cops would cuff him and drag him to a back room where they would proceed to plow his ass until he couldn't stand up. Sadly, this was real life. They were probably relentlessly straight and only here for a beer.

They headed toward the end of the bar by the register where there weren't any customers during the midafternoon lull.

"What can I get for you, officers?" Mason asked.

The big one smiled. "Anything cold."

The shorter man punched his partner's arm. "Nothing. Thank you. We're here on official business."

The big man rolled his eyes. "Can't I at least get a soda?"

"Fine. Two Cokes please."

Mason was glad to have the simple task of scooping ice and pouring fountain drinks to distract himself for a few minutes. What official business would they have here? While the occasional fistfight broke out, most typically during the NCAA basketball tournament, Nathan's Public House was hardly a hotbed of crime.

He picked up the drinks and faced them again, willing his hands to stop shaking. It wasn't like he hadn't served plenty of attractive men in the past. What was it about these two that had him so stirred up?

He set the drinks on the bar in front of them and watched as they both took a sip. His cheeks heated when he realized he was staring, openmouthed, at the flex of muscles in the bigger man's throat as he swallowed.

Focus, Mason, focus. "So…um…what kind of business brings you here?"

The shorter man smiled and held out his hand. "I'm Officer Jack Abney, and this is my partner, Gray Sadler. We want to talk to the staff who were working last night when Gino's was robbed in case anyone might have seen or heard something that will help with the investigation."

Mason took Jack's hand. His skin was softer than Mason expected, and he held Mason's hand a few seconds longer than he needed to. "Um…I'm Mason Shields."

"Nice to meet you, Mr. Shields," Jack said, grinning.

Mason thought he might melt, but this wasn't a time to become a puddle of lustful intentions. The robberies had shaken up most of the business owners in the part of downtown Durham where Nathan's was located. The break-in at Gino's was the third one in the area, and all the robberies were believed to have been inside jobs pulled off by well-organized professionals. The occasional group of kids breaking a window and trying to get into the till or taking valuables customers foolishly left lying on the seats of their cars wasn't uncommon, but this type of systematic criminal activity was something new.

"I was here last night, but until I heard sirens, I had no idea anything was going on. It was really crowded, and I had a long line at the bar so I was focused on making drinks and keeping customers happy."

Jack stood up and looked toward the windows. "Not much of a view of the place either."

Mason shook his head. "Once the lights go out over there, I can't see a thing, especially with people blocking my view out front."

His partner, Officer Sadler, looked at Mason then, his dark eyes calculating. "We understand one of your servers worked at Gino's until a month or so ago."

"Yes, Gwen did." The idea of Gwen working for a band of criminal masterminds was ludicrous. She could barely manage to serve a couple of tables without fucking up their orders.

"Was she working last night?" Gray asked.

Mason thought through the evening. Gwen had been there, but he didn't remember seeing her after the dinner crowd left, and he'd wondered why they were understaffed when the rowdy game watchers filled the place up. "She was, but her shift must have ended by nine."

"Is that unusual?" Jack studied him as carefully as his partner had. Having the two gorgeous men staring at him was doing unsettling things to his insides, and his expanding dick was making his pants uncomfortable.

"I guess so. Kinda. Usually most of the waitstaff works until eleven on weekends, but I really don't think—"

Jack held up his hand. "Just routine questions."

"Okay. Maybe it would be better if you talked to my manager."

"We will," Gray assured him. "But right now, we want to talk to you."

His voice was low and sexy. If Mason didn't know better, he'd have thought Gray was flirting with him, but he had to be imagining it. Jack was staring at his partner like he'd lost his mind.

Mason looked back at Gray and was caught by his cool gaze. He bit into his lip, needing the sharp pain to break the spell and allow him to look away. Gray exuded dominance. Mason had no doubt he was a man who expected to get his way, and Mason would be happy to give him just that. The thought of being pinned under him and told exactly how to please him made Mason shudder.

Needing to break the tension vibrating among the three of them, Mason said, "The bartender knows all, is that the theory?"

"Something like that." Jack's sly grin made Mason's knees weak. These two were going to be the death of him.

The officers asked a few more questions, but Mason truly didn't have anything useful to tell them so they moved on to questioning the servers.

He was glad there weren't many customers in the bar because both cops had asses worthy of his devoted attention. He sighed as he watched them while pretending to wipe down the bar. What he wouldn't give to peel them out of their tight blue pants and get a closer look.

The intensity of his attraction puzzled Mason. Gray's size and dominating presence pushed all his buttons, setting off submissive fantasies that had him reeling. And Jack, Mason could imagine him reveling in a hard, rough fuck or giving the orders himself with the confident air he used for interrogation. If the two men had told him to drop his pants and bend over the bar, he truly might have done it, which unnerved him. While he'd had his share of hook-up sex with no names exchanged, he wasn't usually quite so slutty.

Maybe the fact that it had been months since he'd bothered to find a partner at all was part of the problem. He'd never really enjoyed the anonymous club sex, but he'd learned the hard way that depending on someone to be there for you was pointless, so he wasn't much for relationships either. Hitting the clubs was the easiest way to take care of his sexual urges. He'd stepped out of his comfort zone often enough to keep from dying of unfulfilled lust, but the last few times he'd hooked up with someone in a grungy bathroom, he'd felt more sick than satisfied after it was over. For the last few months, he'd reveled in his nerdy side, the side of him that still hoped to go back to college, get his degree in chemistry, and then move on to grad school. Instead of going out he'd been spending his time off reading scientific journals and watching his favorite *Star Trek* episodes over and over. Perhaps he was experiencing temporary insanity from lack of sex.

Chapter Two

Over the next few weeks, Jack and Gray became frequent customers at Nathan's, and Mason never got tired of watching them. He often caught them giving each other appreciative glances, and while most of their casual touches fell within acceptable limits for straight-male camaraderie, their expressions were more tender than he would expect from hardened cops. He'd nearly convinced himself they were more than friends. Every time he saw something that hinted that they were lovers, he scolded himself for wishful thinking, but that didn't prevent fantasizing about the two of them rubbing their naked, sweaty bodies against each other from becoming his favorite pastime. Jack and Gray had inspired a full-on cop fetish.

One night, the two cops came in when their shift ended. After eating dinner, they ordered dessert—tiramisu, Mason's favorite. During a break in taking orders, Mason watched Gray stab his fork into the confection and then proceed to lick at it like it was a lollipop. It was the most erotic thing Mason had ever seen. Every swipe of Gray's tongue made his cock throb. Finally, panting and painfully hard, he forced himself to turn away and think about things that were sure to make him lose his erection—disposing of the mouse traps he'd placed under the kitchen sink in his apartment or the dishwasher who'd started working at Nathan's last week who had apparently never heard of deodorant.

When even those thoughts didn't deflate him, he knew he had a serious problem. He didn't have a break for several hours, and even if he could slip away, was he really going to jerk off in a bathroom stall at work like he was sixteen? He needed to get a grip. Clearly he'd been a recluse too long, but if he went clubbing with this obsession riding him, he would end up comparing every man he danced with to Gray and Jack. Chances were, he would find them all lacking.

"Bring me another round, Mason." A shout from Chris, one of the regulars, interrupted his reverie.

Mason had already served him a slew of drinks, and he looked ready to slide off his barstool. "You've had enough. Let me call you a cab."

"Fuck no. The last place I want to be is home."

Mason sighed. Chris's girlfriend had found a new love interest a few weeks ago, and Mason didn't think the man had been sober since.

"You've wallowed long enough," Mason replied. "Go home, get some sleep, and start over tomorrow."

Chris shook his head. "I just don't get it."

Mason took a slow breath. The man had really thought the girl he'd been dating was The One. Mason believed she had just been looking for someone who'd pay for her drinks and buy her gifts, but he hadn't told Chris that. Chris's drama was wearing thin on him. The lending-a-sympathetic-ear part of bartending did not come naturally to Mason.

He'd much rather contemplate the chemistry behind mixing the perfect cocktail than chat with customers, but he'd needed a decent-paying job. When his friend who'd had the job before him finished his degree, he'd put in a good word for Mason. Elizabeth, the manager who'd bought the bar from Nathan himself, agreed to hire him despite his lack of experience. He learned quickly and impressed Elizabeth so much that she made him assistant manager.

He turned away from Chris to take an order from a pink-haired girl who didn't look sixteen, much less twenty-one. As he asked for her ID, he saw Chris's ex, Heather, walk through the door, arm wrapped around the waist of her new man. He sighed. Chris was going to make an ass of himself at the very least, and wind up spending the night in jail at worst. He looked for Jack and Gray, but they no longer occupied the corner table.

He checked the ID of the youngster, which appeared to be real. After he made her a rum and Coke, he glanced back at Chris, who still hadn't noticed his ex. She was cozied up to the man she was with and petting him every chance she got. Mason took a deep breath and focused on making more drinks, ignoring the nasty looks Chris was giving him for not bringing him one.

A few minutes later, after taking drinks to a few tables for waitresses who were too overworked to keep up, Mason heard raised voices from the far end of the bar. Heather had come over to Chris's table to say hello. Was she trying to start a fight?

He rang up a customer who was ready to pay his tab while continually glancing toward Chris and watching the situation escalate as Heather's new boyfriend got in on the action. When Mason had given the customer his change, he looked toward Chris and cringed. He was off his stool confronting the boyfriend. Punches were going to start flying any second.

Mason held up a finger to indicate he'd be right back to help the next person in line and made his way over to Chris. He came around the bar and laid a hand on the man's shoulder. "Let me call you a cab."

"Fucking bastard says I stole his girl," the boyfriend said, looking like he was itching to knock Chris on his fool ass.

"Why don't y'all find a table, and I'll bring you some drinks on the house." Mason was desperate to diffuse the situation.

Heather and her boyfriend started to walk off, but when he slid his hand down her back and squeezed her ass, Chris lost it. He grabbed the man by the shoulder, turned him around, and punched him. Mason doubted Chris was even really angry with the new boyfriend. It was Heather who'd come over and flaunted him in Chris's face, but while Chris might be an ass sometimes, he would never hit a woman so her boyfriend got it instead.

The guy returned the punch, and Chris staggered, falling against the bar then springing back up, ready to keep going. Mason tried to pull him back, but he charged the other man like a bull going for a matador.

Everyone in the bar turned to watch the fight. If they were in a Wild West saloon, Mason would have fired his gun into the air to scare the brawlers. As it was, he shouted at them with no effect.

Relief hit when he saw Jack pushing his way through the gathering crowd. He'd thought the two cops had already left, but they must have vacated their booth and headed for the pool tables or dart boards.

Mason made one last attempt to pull Chris back. "You're about to get yourself arrested," he yelled as he tugged at Chris's arm. Chris shoved him, and Mason fell against the bar.

"You okay?" Jack asked.

Mason nodded then Jack whistled. The sharp sound startled the two men who were fighting. The boyfriend's eyes widened when he took note of Jack's uniform, but Chris was too far gone to pay attention to what was happening. He pulled back to sink another punch, and Jack grabbed his arm. Chris spun and punched him in the face.

Mason winced. Now Chris was really fucked. Mason should have sent him home much earlier.

Chris's eyes were wide, crazed, and Mason wondered if he'd been doing more than drinking. Chris yanked himself from Jack's hold and charged the boyfriend, who'd tried to back away but hadn't been able to get very far because of the crowd.

"Chris," Mason shouted. The man glanced toward him, and Mason threw a well-timed punch. Chris slumped to the ground and didn't move. Mason turned to see Jack staring at him in surprise. Mason was small, but he had taken self-defense classes years ago as a scrawny gay teen after the first time he was beaten up. He'd sworn he'd never let himself be that defenseless again, and he hadn't.

Before Jack had a chance to say anything, Gray came barreling toward them, making on-lookers scatter. "Is everything ok here?"

Jack turned to his partner. The look on Gray's face when he saw Jack's black eye confirmed Mason's suspicions; the two men were more than work partners. Gray looked like a vengeful archangel, ready to rip apart anyone who dared harm the man he loved. He laid a hand on Jack's arm, then pulled it back quickly like he had something to hide.

"Got the jump on you, did he?" Gray asked, tough cop façade back in place.

Jack shrugged. "I overestimated my calming charm, but our favorite bartender saved me."

Favorite? Did he really just say I was his favorite?

Gray looked at Mason then, his gazing sliding up and down as if once again he'd forgotten where he was. How hard would it be to play the macho cop when you loved your partner? While there were plenty of things Mason disliked about his job, at least he could be himself.

"Did he now?" Gray's low resonating voice sent a shiver through Mason.

"Chris was running down. I just gave him the nudge he needed to end things."

Gray looked down at the still-unconscious man. "Don't ever nudge me like that."

Mason smiled sheepishly. "No, I…wouldn't…. I just…"

Gray saved him from needing to speak by laying one of his enormous hands on Mason's shoulder. "Thank you."

"You're welcome. I…um…better get back to serving drinks."

Jack and Gray nodded.

Mason slipped behind the bar as Gray knelt to put cuffs around Chris's wrists. Chris roused but didn't fully wake. Gray tossed the semi-conscious man over his shoulder while Jack worked to disperse the crowd and clear a path to the door.

Mason had to force himself not to stare at Gray's and Jack's fine asses as they left. They were truly some of the hottest men he'd ever seen. If only…no, he was more certain than ever that they were a couple. They were also customers. And Mason didn't need to get involved with anyone at Nathan's. The sexy cops needed to remain in the realm of fantasy.

Chapter Three

The night after the bar fight, Jack and Gray came into Nathan's and sat at a corner table. Mason tried to work up the nerve to talk to them while he was on break, but they looked so intimate sitting there together. Their connection wasn't something most people would notice, but now that he was certain there was more between them than friendship, their gestures and the way they looked at each other were telling. He wondered if the other guys on the force knew they were gay. If so, surely they didn't realize the men were lovers. They wouldn't be allowed to be partners then, would they?

Jack caught Mason staring once and winked at him. Heat crept up Mason's neck and into his face, and he looked away. But when he worked up the nerve to sneak another glance at them, he caught Jack watching him. His gaze drifted up and down, pointedly checking Mason out. Mason grinned and waved even though his hand was shaking. He was playing with fire, especially if Gray was the jealous type. Mason might be able to knock Chris to the ground, but Gray could snap Mason in two like a twig.

He wondered about the nature of Jack and Gray's relationship. Were they exclusive? They certainly looked like they were more than just a convenient fuck for each other. But what was up with them flirting with him? Even if he'd misread Gray's comments the day they questioned him, he couldn't deny that Jack was flirting with him that night. Did Jack want him? Did they both? The thought of a three-way with the two of them was almost more than he could stand. Trying to ignore those dangerous thoughts, he made himself busy straightening the little trays of fruits and olives to add to drinks.

Later that night when Mason was alone in bed, hand wrapped around his cock, bringing himself some relief from the stress of the day, he couldn't get the officers out of his head. He let his favorite fantasy play out. Gray had him tied up. The big man toyed with Mason, tormented him, then watched as Jack fucked him. Then it was his turn, and he was driving into Mason, fucking him relentlessly, telling Mason he owned him. Mason shuddered and climaxed with the image of Gray leaning over him, face contorted with his own orgasm, emblazoned on his brain.

Getting involved with Jack and Gray was a bad idea. They could easily become an obsession, and Mason had learned better than to sleep with couples. He shuddered as he thought about Brett and Andrew and the disaster sleeping with them turned out to be.

Mason had just come out to his family and gotten the reaction he'd expected. His mother had berated him for his shocking lack of social tact in choosing to sleep with men, and his father had counseled him not to tell anyone else while he worked through this wild phase. His sister had sided with both of them, kissing up as usual. Mason was feeling more alone than he ever had, and when Brett, the TA in one of his chemistry classes with whom he'd bonded over their mutual *Battlestar Galactica* obsession, propositioned him after the final exam, he had no power to resist. He went home with Brett and let the man fuck him senseless. They saw each other several more times over the next few weeks, then Brett told him he had a boyfriend.

Mason was horrified, but Brett assured him he and Andrew had an open relationship and asked if he was up for a three-way. Mason was nervous as hell, but he agreed. The evening was amazing, and so was the next one, and the next. They spent most of a long weekend in bed. Then one morning, Mason woke up to the sound of Andrew railing at Brett, telling him he knew Brett liked fucking Mason better. Mason sneaked out the door while they argued.

Andrew had come to Mason's apartment later that day and threatened him, telling him he'd make him pay if he didn't stay away from Brett. The next day, Brett called saying he'd broken up with Andrew. Brett had started harassing Mason, begging him to go out with him.

In his anxiety over that disaster, Mason threw himself at a much older man he met at a sci-fi con, a man he realized later was more in need of a housekeeper than a boyfriend. He'd thought their relationship had real potential, that maybe he was in love with the man, but when Mason's father announced that he wouldn't pay for school anymore if Mason didn't plan to attend law school after graduation, his boyfriend proved to be unwilling to consider any needs other than his own. His job suddenly took up all his time, and he ended up telling Mason to pull himself together and get over it or they were done. Mason had never spoken to him again. So yeah, Mason had good reason to be shy of relationships and of couples who claimed to want to play around with someone else. But sometimes, being alone really sucked.

*****

One slow afternoon a few days later, Jack and Gray walked in and sat down at the bar. They were in uniform, and the sight of them sent a shiver through Mason. He took a deep breath before walking over with a pounding heart and sweaty palms to take their order.

"Thanks for your help the other night," Gray said before Mason had a chance to speak. Gray's eyes were as mesmerizing as usual, but today they looked warmer than they had before. Mason couldn't look away from him. He licked his lips then his face heated as he realized how revealing the gesture was.

"No problem. I'm just sorry he got a punch in before we brought him down."

Jack smiled. "I'm fine. It's not the first time, and it won't be last. Are you working late today?"

Jack's question surprised Mason so much he almost dropped the glass he'd been fiddling with. "Um…yeah, I work till closing."

Gray gave Mason an assessing glance that made Mason's cock start to swell. What would it be like for Gray to look at him like that when they were both naked? He busied himself wiping down the bar and tried to ignore how much he wanted these two gorgeous men. But surely they were just enjoying a little harmless flirtation. He couldn't read more into it.

"We'd love to get a drink some time," Gray said.

Drinks. Yeah, he was a bartender and they were here to order drinks, not to cozy up to him. "Sorry, what would you like?"

Jack caught his hand and pinned it to the bar. "No, the three of us, somewhere else, when you're not working. We'd like to have a drink *together*."

"Oh!" Mason was certain his cheeks were as red as the maraschino cherries he used to decorate drinks. "That kind of drink?"

Gray chuckled. "Yeah. That kind." The words came out slow, seductive.

Mason's dick hardened more. "I…um…aren't you two…?"

Jack grinned at Mason's stumbling attempt to make sure he understood what they wanted. "We are, but we both like you."

Mason thought he might pass out from the lack of blood going to his brain. *Danger, danger!* his mind screamed, but his cock was not listening.

Gray captured his hand as Jack let go. He pressed his thumb into Mason's wrist, stroking firmly. Mason thought he might honest-to-God swoon.

"Or…" Gray paused and Mason waited, heart thundering in his ears. "We could just skip the drink."

Mason sucked in his breath. His ears rang and his vision went dark at the edges. There was no way he'd be able to resist these men, no matter how much he knew better.

"Gray, don't push," Jack said, obviously holding back a laugh.

"I think he likes being pushed," Gray responded. He tightened his fingers around Mason's wrist. "If I told you where to meet us, you'd be there, wouldn't you?"

"Yes." The word came out in a breathy rush.

Gray smiled. "Would you like it if I just took control and didn't give you a choice?"

Mason didn't think his dick had ever been that hard. For years he'd fantasized about having a man dominate him, control him, punish him. But the one time he'd gone to a BDSM club, he couldn't get past the leather and collars; it was too much for him. He wanted dominance without all the trappings. He'd left before he even talked to anyone. But Gray was exactly what he'd been looking for. "Um…I—"

Jack's radio buzzed. A message came through filled with codes Mason didn't understand. Jack glanced at Gray. "We've got to go."

Gray nodded. Then he grabbed a napkin and handed it to Mason. "Write your number down."

Mason grabbed a pen from the cup by the register and scrawled his number on the napkin. He handed it to Gray, who made a point of letting his fingers brush across the back of Mason's hand. The contact sent shivers through Mason.

Mason tried to think of something else to say but once Gray pocketed his number, the two men took off, leaving Mason staring at the door. Had they really propositioned him? Would he really do whatever Gray told him to despite his no-couples rule?

He'd be crazy to turn down what promised to be mind-blowing sex, yet his cops belonged firmly in the world of fantasy. Sex with them might just kill him, and the potential for drama was too high. They were a couple and he was in danger of wanting far more from them than a one-night stand. This was a very bad idea.

He sighed. Maybe they wouldn't call. Their asking for his number might have been the result of temporary insanity. Was there a full moon? He'd just wait and see and fantasize and obsess and long to feel their hands on him. Oh fuck, he was in so much trouble.

Chapter Four

The next day, one of the regulars told Mason there'd been another robbery a few streets over from the bar. Mason didn't hear from Jack and Gray, but he hadn't expected to since they were working the robbery case. The only excitement in his day was getting into an argument with the idiotic waitress, Gwen, after he caught her sneaking a cigarette in the office when he went in to put the money from the bar till in the safe.

The following day was his day off. He heard his phone ring, but he was in line at the grocery store so he ignored it. When he pulled it out of his pocket after he got home, he saw that he'd missed a call from an unknown number. There was no voice mail.

The number was local. Could it be Gray or Jack? Did he dare call back to find out?

He pressed redial before he could talk himself out of it.

"You working tonight?" Gray's voice. Obviously he didn't go in for social niceties on the phone.

"No. It's my day off."

"Good. Meet us at Undertow at nine."

"Okay, I—"

"Gotta go."

Fitting In

Gray ended the call, and Mason stood there in his kitchen with the phone to his ear for several seconds. Had that just happened?

*****

That night, Mason found a spot in the employee parking lot by Nathan's. He wasn't supposed to use the lot when he wasn't working, but most likely no one would notice. Undertow was a gay-friendly dive bar located a few blocks away from Nathan's. He'd only been there a few times, mostly on Thursdays when a local chef who was hoping to get his own restaurant one day took over the kitchen and served Ethiopian food.

As he walked, he wished he'd worn a heavier coat. The early March wind cut right through his jacket. At least he could pretend he was shivering from cold rather than nerves. He laughed as he always did when he saw the sign at the top of the stairs leading to Undertow's entrance. "Undertow. We'll suck you right down."

He pulled open the door and stepped inside, wishing his heart wasn't thundering against his chest. He briefly contemplated turning around and running like the coward he was.

The room was a long rectangle with a high ceiling and exposed ducts. The bar took up much of the front part of the room. The back opened up for more seating and a pool table. He scanned the tables and located Jack and Gray in a booth just past the end of the bar. Gray acknowledged him with a slow perusal and a smile. Mason pointed toward the bar, indicating that he would get a drink and then join them. He wasn't sure he'd be able to drink anything though. Butterflies were performing gymnastic routines in his stomach.

He ordered a Cape Cod, but when he reached for it, his hand was so sweaty he nearly dropped the glass. What was he playing at? He was a nerdy guy who wanted to be a chemist and read scientific articles for fun. A three-way with a couple of closeted cops was so not his speed. At least most of his previous idiotic decisions had involved nerdy guys like himself.

Jack slid over, making room for Mason on his side of the booth. "Glad you made it," he said, letting his hand rest on Mason's arm.

"Um…yeah. Me too." He looked from one of them to the other. Jack was wearing a black t-shirt and a black leather jacket. He looked like the captain of the football team playing the part of a bad boy.

"Like what you see?" Jack asked, grinning at him.

Mason looked into his sky blue eyes and couldn't remember how to talk.

"He does," Gray said, his deep voice calling to Mason, breaking the spell Jack held on him. He looked at Gray and Jack let his hand drop to Mason's thigh. He slid it back and forth, caressing him through his jeans. His fingers came within inches of Mason's cock, which was now very interested in the proceedings.

"Jack, how can we talk to him with you doing that?" Gray asked.

Jack grinned. "I can't wait any longer. I've been wanting to touch him for so long."

Gray raised his brows. "He is quite tempting, but you're distracting him."

Mason sat, paralyzed. He looked back and forth between them as they talked about him, unable to do anything but enjoy the sensation of Jack's hand on his thigh, the heat of his touch seeping into Mason's skin.

Jack squeezed his leg and let go, bringing his hands up on the table and lacing them together. "See? I'm going to be good now," he said to Gray.

Gray snorted. But before he could say anything else, a woman slipped out through the kitchen doors and brought a plate of Undertow's famous bacon-wrapped dates to their table.

"Thank you," Gray said in his sultry voice.

"You're welcome," she responded, blushing fiercely, obviously as much under Gray's spell as Mason was.

"Gray can't resist these," Jack explained as the server walked away.

Gray grinned, looking like a kid with candy rather than an intimidating cop.

They each bit into one of the salty-sweet treats, groaning and muttering their appreciation of the culinary marvel.

Mason, able to talk again now that Jack wasn't touching him, asked them the question that had been on his mind since they'd asked him to meet them. "So you don't mind being seen together here"—he looked down to where Jack was now stroking the back of his hand, his "goodness" only having lasted a short time—"with me?"

Gray shrugged. "No one here cares."

Jack looked uncomfortable. He started to say something, but Gray glared at him. Mason could tell he'd hit a nerve. Obviously, they didn't agree on what level of risk they should take.

"You're not out at work, are you?" Mason asked.

Jack shook his head. "We're not. We can't be, but apparently Gray doesn't care anymore if we get caught."

Gray sighed. "I care...I just—"

"He insisted we move in together."

"We told everyone Jack couldn't find another roommate when the guy he'd been living with got married. I said I needed help with my rent and so I asked him to move in with me. It's convenient."

Jack rolled his eyes. "Yeah, it's convenient for you to have me in your bed every night."

Gray smiled. "Damn right."

Jack blew out a long, slow breath. "Sorry. It's hard on both of us, but even if we were prepared to take the flack we'd get—the butt-sex jokes, the guys who would refuse to work with us—we wouldn't be able to be partners anymore."

Gray nodded. "And that would suck. We're good together."

Jack smiled at him, utter devotion plain on his face. "At work and at home."

Mason's chest tightened. No one who saw the look they gave each other would doubt that they were in love. He had no business messing around with them and risking making either of them jealous.

He started to slide from the booth, but Jack grabbed his leg again. "We're nowhere near done with you."

Gray gave him a look that made his heart skip a beat. "Definitely not. I have a lot of plans for you."

"But you two are…."

Jack patted his leg. "We like you, remember?"

"And you like us too," Gray said, his low, rich voice sliding over Mason like a caress.

"But I don't want to come between you."

Gray laughed. "I'd enjoy you cumming between us." His tone made his double entendre clear.

Mason choked on his drink, and Jack rolled his eyes at Gray as he patted Mason's back. "You're worried because Gray and I are together?"

Mason nodded. "I was with a couple once and things…ended badly."

Jack pushed Mason's hair off his face and ran his fingers through it. Mason couldn't stop himself from leaning into Jack's touch. "Gray and I have talked about this. There's something about you, something we both want," Jack said.

They weren't Brett and Andrew; Mason had to acknowledge that. They seemed much more mature, but he was still terrified.

Silence settled over the table, and Mason felt the need to fill it. "Did you always want to be cops?"

Gray nodded, but he didn't elaborate.

"As a kid, I didn't really think too much about the future," Jack said. "I figured I'd go to college, and eventually, I'd figure out what I wanted to do. Then when I was sixteen, my parents had gone out for the evening, and my younger brother and I were home by ourselves. Two men broke in. I grabbed my phone and crawled out my window as I called 911. I intended to get my brother out through his bedroom window, but he'd gotten up to go to the bathroom, and the men had seen him. They were holding him at gunpoint.

"I'd never been so scared in my life. But before I did something stupid like running in to try and save him, the police got there. They talked the men down and saved my brother. I decided that night that I was going to be a cop. I wanted to be able to help people the way they'd helped us. I guess, in a way, I thought I owed the world for my brother's survival."

Mason reached for Jack's hand and squeezed it. Jack squeezed back and smiled.

"How did you two meet?" Mason asked.

Gray looked uncomfortable, but Jack answered eagerly. "Gray came in to assist in a class when I was at the academy. We did a fight simulation together, and I could tell that he liked me—a lot."

Gray scowled. "I'd never gotten hard teaching that class before."

"Your body was just telling you I was the one." Gray snorted.

Jack ignored him and turned to Mason. "So what about you? How did you end up at Nathan's?"

Mason felt heat rise into his face. "Compared to your story, it's very mundane."

"Doesn't matter," Gray said. "We want to get to know you."

Mason realized he wanted to get to know them too, and that was a scary feeling for someone who'd taught himself to do without romantic relationships. "The short version of the story is that I needed the money."

"And the longer version?" Jack asked.

"Before I started my last year at Duke, I told my parents that I didn't want to go to law school. They might have accepted it if I'd wanted to go to med school instead, and if I were straight I might could even have gotten away with business or engineering, but a plain old chemistry degree just wasn't going to cut it. They told me I could either continue with the pre-law track or they wouldn't pay for my school anymore. I dropped out, and a friend got me the job at Nathan's. That was two years ago. I want to go back to school once I've saved enough, but for now…." Mason shrugged.

Jack shook his head. "Your parents accepted you being gay, but they couldn't accept you making your own career choice?"

Mason laughed but the sound was bitter. "They believed, actually they still do believe, that I'll get over 'the gay thing'. Refusing to follow the career path they set for me was the final straw. I'm not the man they want me to be, a straight lawyer with conservative political leanings. They're still operating under the delusion that I'll eventually 'see sense' and marry one of their friends' daughters."

Gray leaned back in the booth and assessed him. "Have you ever let a man tie you up?"

Mason sputtered. That was one hell of a subject change. "N-no."

"But you'd like to, wouldn't you?"

"Gray," Jack warned.

Mason would like it. Very much. "Yeah, I think so, I mean…yeah."

Gray gave Jack a look that said "I told you so".

Jack cupped the back of Mason's neck and kneaded. Jack's touch felt so good that Mason bit his lip to keep from moaning.

Gray's eyes darkened as he held Mason's gaze. "We play safe. If you want us to stop, we'll stop, but I'd love to see if you'd enjoy submitting as much as I think you will."

"Oh my God." The words slipped out before Mason could stop them.

Jack slid his fingers into Mason's hair and massaged the back of his head. This time Mason didn't stop his moan from escaping.

"So responsive," Jack whispered.

"Beautiful," Gray said.

Mason realized he'd closed his eyes and sunk into Jack's touch, letting the man transport him away from the noisy bar. Heat filled his cheeks. He hadn't meant to get so carried away. What was it about these men that made him trust them so easily?

"I have a surprise planned for you." Gray's words went straight to Mason's cock, making it press even harder against his fly.

"Gray," Jack used his warning tone again.

"You know he'll love it," Gray said, dismissing his concern.

"A surprise?" Mason asked.

"You'd like that, wouldn't you?"

Mason's heart pounded. Why did he feel like he was making a deal with the devil? "I-I guess."

"Oh, you will. Just wait."

Jack ran his hand along Mason's arm. "Are we ready to go?" he asked.

Gray nodded and stood. Jack pushed gently on Mason's shoulder, and he stood on shaky legs. Somehow he managed to follow Gray to the door and up to street level.

Jack watched Mason like he wanted to devour him, but he didn't touch him now that they'd left the relative safety of the bar.

"I'm parked back at Nathan's," Mason said.

"We're across the street." Gray tilted his head toward a large pay lot. "We'll drive you to your car."

They walked to Gray's black SUV in silence. Gray unlocked the doors, and Mason got into the back seat. Rather than getting into the front with Gray, Jack climbed into the back with Mason.

"You two behave back there," Gray said, his voice stern but his eyes bright and mischievous.

Jack laughed. "Not a chance."

As Gray backed out, Jack reached for Mason and pulled him in for a kiss. Jack tasted like the dark beer he'd been drinking, but also like something wild and forbidden. Mason couldn't get enough. He took Jack's face in his hands and held him so he couldn't escape. Their tongues tangled, reaching, pushing, sliding along each other. Jack pulled Mason's shirt from his pants and pushed his hands underneath, sliding them up Mason's back and practically crawling on top of him. By the time they reached Nathan's, Mason and Jack were both panting.

Gray whistled. "Time's up."

Jack climbed off Mason's lap and the two men stared at each other in the dim light shining into the car from the streetlights.

"We'll see you soon," Gray said.

A few seconds passed before Gray's words sank in. He wasn't being asked back to their house. "But…I thought…."

"You thought you'd get your surprise tonight." Gray gave a low, evil chuckle. "No. I want you anticipating it. I want you so horny from fantasizing about us that you think you'll die if you don't have us."

"I think I'm already there."

Jack laughed. "You obviously have no idea how far Gray can push you."

Mason groaned and ran a hand through his hair.

"Don't worry. We won't make you wait too long. Will we, Gray?"

Gray turned and captured Mason's gaze. "You have my word you'll get what we've promised. Just not tonight."

"But—"

"Are you questioning me, boy?"

Mason sucked in his breath. None of his partners, even the ones who'd been several years older, had ever called him boy or spoken to him with such command in their voice. "N-no."

"Good. Be careful driving home. And don't even think about touching yourself. The next time you come will be when I tell you to."

Mason's mouth dropped open. "Are you serious?" he asked.

Gray glared. "Very."

Later that night, Mason barely remembered getting out of the SUV and getting into his own car. As he drove home, he couldn't shake the idea that the whole evening had been a dream. No one was really as fucking sexy as Gray and Jack, at least not anyone who wanted him.

Chapter Five

The next night, Mason chased out the stragglers who'd hung on until last call. The servers had helped him put the chairs up on the tables, sweep, and wipe down the bar. When most of the final chores were done, he sent everyone else home. He only had to take out the trash, then he could lock the back door, head home, and crash. It had been a long damn day.

Thoughts of Jack and Gray had kept him semi-hard almost constantly. He'd almost masturbated the night before. How would Gray know whether he had or not? But when he remembered the look in Gray's eyes as he'd assured Mason he was very serious about his order, Mason had stopped himself. He'd slept like shit, dreaming of the two hot men, and now he wished to hell he hadn't denied himself.

As he swung the heavy trash bags up through the sliding door of the dumpster behind the bar, headlights flashed across the alley, and a car pulled into the tiny parking lot beside the bar. Probably someone heading to the diner down the street. He ignored it. The last thing he cared about was trying to enforce the customer-parking-only rule after closing. He headed inside and locked the back door behind him.

But before he could grab his messenger bag from the break room, someone banged on the front door. When he headed back to the dining area, he saw someone shining a flashlight into the bar. The knock came again. "Police, open up."

It sounded like Gray, and as Mason got closer, he recognized the tall man's silhouette. He raced across the room and opened the door.

"What's going on?" he asked.

"Step back inside, sir. We got a call that there was someone at this address who needed to be taught a lesson."

Taught a lesson? What did he mean, and why was he acting like they hadn't met?

Gray brushed past him and walked into the bar, shining his flashlight toward the kitchen, then walking the perimeter of the room. Mason watched him, still trying to figure out what was going on.

"What have you been up to here, sir?" Gray asked.

Had the man gone crazy? "Um...I'm just closing up. I don't understand."

"Are you sure that's all, sir? Are you sure there's not something...untoward...going on here?" Gray pitched his voice low and drew his words out, stirring something in Mason. Oh my God, maybe they were strippers like he'd thought at first. No, that was crazy. They were real cops, but real cops didn't play games like this. They—

Someone came up behind him and laid his hands on Mason's shoulders. Mason jerked away before he realized it was Jack. Even without seeing him, Mason recognized his scent, the musky cologne he liked to wear mixed with sweat and something primal that just smelled like Jack. Jack grabbed him again, spinning him around and pinning his arms behind his back. Mason shuddered as Jack's hands tightened around his wrists. Hot, driving lust rushed through him, his need battling with the sensible side of him that said he should be in a full-scale panic right now. These men could easily overpower him. But Jack wouldn't really hurt him. This was just a game. Surely.

As if he'd read Mason's thoughts, Jack leaned forward, his lips brushing the outer edge of Mason's ear. "Say the word and I'll let you go. We just want to have some fun if you're up to it."

Mason glanced over his shoulder at Jack. He couldn't make his voice work, but Jack's smile reassured him.

"Just closing up and nothing more? A likely story," Gray said, walking toward them.

Mason shivered. Gray looked ferocious, and every step he took showed off the power in his body.

He stopped right in front of Mason and looked him up and down. "You're under arrest."

Mason swore he could feel Gray's low, sexy voice in his chest. He couldn't stop the protest that spilled from his lips. "But I haven't done anything."

Gray arched a brow and glared at him. "Are you resisting?"

Am I?

Mason swallowed and forced himself to meet Gray's steely gaze. "No, sir. I'm not resisting."

Gray smiled and Mason saw the man behind the façade for just a second. "Good. I like a boy who can take his punishment."

Mason sucked in his breath. His dick was now impossibly hard. If Jack hadn't been restraining him he would have pinched himself to make sure he wasn't dreaming.

Mason felt the cold metal of handcuffs brush against his wrist. "Is this what you want?" Jack asked.

He nodded.

Jack tugged his arms together and snapped the cuffs around his wrists. "Do you have a safeword?" he asked, his warm breath tickling Mason's ear.

Mason shook his head.

"Say red, and we'll stop, no questions asked. This is all about pleasure."

"Okay." The word came out in a barely audible whisper.

Jack ran his tongue along the outer edge of Mason's ear, making him shiver. "Gray and I are both clean. We get tested regularly. We go bareback with each other, but when we play with someone else, we always use condoms. If anything we want makes you uncomfortable, you tell us right away. You got that?"

He nodded again.

"What's that, boy?" Gray moved forward until he was inches away from Mason. If he took a deep breath, the front of his dark blue uniform shirt would brush against Mason's thin black t-shirt.

Mason swallowed. "Y-yes."

Gray gripped Mason's chin in one of his huge hands, and Mason made an embarrassing sound, a combination of a yelp and a whimper. Gray's hand was warm, almost hot, and Mason shuddered as Gray caressed his jaw with his calloused thumb.

"When we ask you a question, you answer respectfully," Gray said.

"Yes, sir."

The big man smiled. "Much better."

Gray ran his fingers along Mason's neck, across his chest and abdomen, down to his waistband. He hooked his fingers in and pulled, bringing their bodies together.

"Have you been a bad boy?" Gray asked, leering at him, a parody of every cop-themed porn scenario Mason had ever seen.

"N-no, sir."

Gray raised a brow. "Don't lie to me, boy."

"I think he's been very, very bad," Jack purred, resting his hands on Mason's hips and pulling him back so he could feel Jack's erection.

Gray nodded. "Sure he has. Teasing us with all the shy, sexy glances when we're in the bar. Watching us with those bright green eyes, watching but never giving us a clear signal."

"Mmmhmm. Very naughty," Jack agreed. He licked and nipped at the sensitive flesh just behind Mason's ear as he ground against him. "We're going to show him what we do to naughty boys, aren't we?"

"Yes, we are," Gray responded.

"Oh my God." Mason wasn't sure he'd survive.

"Are you scared, boy?" Gray asked, still holding Mason against him, his hard cock brushing against Mason's. If Gray felt this good through clothes, what would it be like to be naked with him?

Mason was afraid he was going to come in his pants if both men kept rubbing on him. Being caught between them was even hotter than he'd imagined.

"You should be," Jack said, trailing kisses down Mason's neck.

Mason shivered, and goose bumps rose along the side of his body.

"Take him to the car," Gray barked as he let go of Mason and stepped away. "I'll get his things. Is your bag in the break room?"

Mason nodded.

"Do you have anything else?"

"A brown coat and my bike's around back. The key to the bike lock is in the front pocket of my bag." Mason was shocked that he'd been able to get all those words out as worked up as he was.

"Biking around at this time of night isn't safe," Gray said, and Mason saw real concern on his face.

"My car's a piece of shit. It only works off and on, and it wouldn't start this morning."

"I'll see what I can do about that," Gray responded. He walked off before Mason could question him. Was he really offering to fix Mason's car? They hardly knew each other.

"Are you good with walking out like this?" Jack asked, tugging on his handcuffs.

Mason considered the question for a few seconds. There hadn't been anyone around when he taken the trash out, so he doubted anyone would see him, and the thrill of being taken away in cuffs by these two incredible men was worth the risk. "I need to lock up," he said. "The key is in my right front pocket."

Jack slid his hand over Mason's hip and pushed into his pocket. He brushed his fingers against Mason's erection before closing them around the key. Mason sucked in his breath as Jack teased him some more, just the barest touch with a single finger, but it was making him crazy.

Gray came back into the room then, carrying Mason bag. He glared at them. "Quit playing around and get him out of here," he barked.

"I had to get the key. We couldn't leave the bar unlocked," Jack purred.

"Get your hand out of his pants right now," Gray said as he walked out the door, not looking back.

Jack did as he was told. He pulled Mason through the doorway, locked up, and then frog-marched Mason to a black SUV that sat at the back of the adjacent parking lot. Mason realized it must be the vehicle he'd seen pulling in when he took out the trash. Jack held Mason's arms as he opened the back door as if he thought he might actually flee like a real prisoner. If Mason had good sense, he would, but he was too far gone with need to even try. He had to find out what they had planned for him. They were bringing his fantasy to life and he was running with it, to hell with the consequences.

"If I take these off so you can sit more comfortably, are you going to behave?" Jack asked, tugging on the cuffs.

"Yes, sir."

"Good. You've got a long night ahead of you. We don't need your arms getting cramped in the car." Jack released the cuffs and then pushed

Mason's head down, maneuvering him into the back seat. Before Jack slammed the door, he leaned down, his face close to Mason's.

Mason froze, thinking Jack was about to kiss him. His gaze fell to Jack's full lips. He needed to taste them again.

"We're taking you back to our house. Are you okay with that?"

Mason had to swallow before he could speak. "Yes."

"Do you remember your safeword?"

Mason raised his gaze to Jack's startlingly blue eyes. "Yes, sir." His voice quavered as he took in the intensity in Jack's eyes.

"Will you use it if you need to?"

"Yes, sir."

"Get in," Gray said, coming up behind Jack and smacking his ass. He'd just finished putting Mason's bike in the back of the SUV.

Jack laughed. "Are you that eager to interrogate our prisoner?"

"Fuck yeah," Gray responded. "I might just interrogate you too."

Jack winked at Mason. "I'm counting on it."

Chapter Six

They left downtown and headed into Old West Durham. After a few minutes, Gray pulled into the driveway of a small, sage green house with cream-colored shutters. The well-kept yard was outlined by a picket fence. The house seemed too delicate for a big, harsh man like Gray, but Mason found the contrast adorable. He loved the idea that there was a lot more to Gray than what he'd seen so far.

Gray opened the back door of the car, and Jack went ahead to unlock their house. A pair of cuffs dangled from Gray's fingers. "Can I trust you without these for now?" he asked.

Mason licked his lips. Part of him wanted to be cuffed, but he wanted to please Gray more and he knew Gray wanted him to be obedient.

"Yes, sir."

"Good. Get out of the car and walk slowly to the house. Follow Jack inside and do as he says. I'll be right behind you."

Mason's heart thundered. He trusted Gray and Jack or he wouldn't be here, but his body was responding as if he were truly in Jack and Gray's power, as if they could do anything to him because no one was watching. The truth was, they could. Cops or not, what he was doing was dangerous, but he wasn't going to stop.

Mason swung his legs from the car and stood, hating the fact that his hands were shaking and his legs were none too steady. He sensed Gray's hulking presence at his back. He longed to sink back into the man or turn around and fall to his knees. But giving a cop a blowjob in front of his house was definitely insane, so Mason forced himself to put one foot in front of the other until he reached the door.

Jack stood in the doorway, grinning. "I think our prisoner is intimidated by you, Gray."

Gray laughed, the sound vibrating through Mason. "He'd damn well should be. I won't be letting him off easy."

Mason shivered as he wondered how far Gray would take his act. Mason had always loved being held down, and he'd let a few lovers tie his hands, but he'd never gone further than light restraints and a few slaps on the ass while he got fucked. As much as he wanted more, he had to admit he was scared.

Jack took his arm and walked him into the center of their living room, a small, comfortable room with a sofa, a recliner that Mason was certain belonged to Gray, and a soft, thick rug over the polished wood floor. Mason glanced down the short hallway that led to the back of the house. One of those doors must lead to the cops' bedroom. Would he soon be spread out on a bed, under one or both of them? His dick sure hoped so.

"Strip," Jack commanded.

Mason heard Gray close and lock the door.

"Now." Jack's voice was sharp, and the usually smiling cop wore a serious expression. He was firmly into his role as interrogator.

Mason's hands shook as he pulled off his t-shirt and dropped it to the floor. He glanced at Jack again. No change in his expression. Mason's heart thundered. Could he really do this?

He sensed Gray moving closer behind him.

"Show me that ass, boy," he commanded.

Mason's hands went to the fastenings of his jeans as he instinctively obeyed Gray's authoritative tone. He unsnapped and unzipped his jeans. He wanted to please Gray by moving quickly, but it was all he could do to push his pants over his hips without falling down. His body vibrated, caught between terror and anticipation. One minute he was asking himself what the hell he was doing there, and the next he was listening to his cock urging him on, telling him to do whatever he needed to get a taste of these men.

When his jeans pooled around his ankles, Gray growled. "You're fucking gorgeous. I'm going to love reddening your ass."

"Oh fuck!" The words slipped out unbidden.

Gray stepped so close Mason could feel his body heat. "If you co-operate and give us the answers we want, maybe you'll get the fuck you need." Gray circled him and looked down pointedly at Mason's cock. It strained upwards toward Gray, the tip glistening with a drop of pre-cum. Mason wanted to beg Gray to touch him. Did the man ever get on his knees?

He looked up and his gaze locked with Gray's. He saw need there and something that looked suspiciously like vulnerability. Was Gray uneasy? Didn't he realize how much Mason wanted this?

"Thank you, sir." He made the words submissive but sensual, and Gray smiled.

Jack had walked out of the room for a few seconds, but he returned carrying a kitchen chair that he placed behind Mason.

Gray laid a hand on Mason's chest right over his breastbone. The heat of his touch sizzled through Mason. He held his breath, waiting for more contact. Gray pushed him, catching him off guard. He stumbled and took a step back.

Jack caught his arm and pulled him down into the seat. "Hands behind your back," he commanded.

Mason did as he said, gaze never leaving Gray, who had gotten something from the coat closet and now loomed over him with a wicked grin on his face as he revealed what was in his hand—a length of inky black rope. He wrapped it around Mason's wrists, and Mason almost purred. It was soft and silken, not scratchy like he'd expect rope to be. Gray tied his hands to the chair tight enough to keep him there, but he wasn't in any pain unless he pulled too hard.

"Don't struggle," Jack said, his voice low and sexy. "We aren't going to let you go."

Mason suppressed a moan. He was probably crazy being here like this with them. He shouldn't trust these men so thoroughly, but he did. Somehow he knew they wouldn't hurt him and that they would stop if he asked.

Jack came around in front of him and knelt. He pulled a leather circle from his pocket. "Have you ever worn a cock ring?"

Mason swallowed hard and shook his head.

"We don't want you coming before we say you can, so I'm going to put it on you. If you're very good, and you prove you can co-operate, Gray will take it off and let you come. You got that?"

Jack held his gaze, and Mason saw concern in his eyes. He could say no, but he didn't want to. He wanted to find out how far this game would go.

Jack lifted Mason's shaft and balls and put the ring in place. Mason's cock throbbed as Jack let him go without touching him more than was necessary to fit the restraint on him. Jack stood and stepped back, and Mason looked up at Gray, ready to beg for his touch.

"Why are you here, boy?"

Mason swallowed and licked his lips, trying to moisten his mouth enough to allow him to speak. "B-because I want you, sir."

Gray chuckled. "Do you now? You see, that's the problem. You'll confess what you want when you're at our mercy, but back at the bar you never once let us know. You just watched us longingly, your cock swelling in your jeans, need plain in your eyes, but never once did you ask. You only teased, letting us see what you wanted but looking away when we caught you staring."

"But I didn't—"

Gray wrapped a hand around Mason's throat, pressing enough for Mason to feel his strength but not enough to hurt him or cut off his air. "Unless I ask you a question, you don't speak. You got that, boy?"

Mason nodded.

Gray raised a brow, squeezing just a little harder.

"Y-yes, sir," Mason whispered.

Gray nodded. "Better. Do you know what happens to bad boys who tease us?"

Mason desperately wanted to know. Gray's roughness had him so turned on he was leaking pre-cum. "No, sir."

Jack walked around and stood behind Gray, wrapping his arms around his lover from behind and rubbing his hands up and down Gray's chest. "Why don't we show him, baby?"

Gray grabbed Jack's hands, stilling them. "We're going to show you what you could have had if you'd asked like a good boy. Then you're going to make a full confession and beg us to bargain with you. You understand, boy?"

Mason started to nod but stopped himself. "Yes, sir."

Gray leaned down again. He breathed deeply right against Mason's neck, but he still didn't touch him. He blew in Mason's ear, then shifted position so his mouth was poised over Mason's nipple. Mason could feel Gray's body heat and he tensed, expecting Gray to bite down on the sensitive pucker, but Gray surprised him. He stayed right where he was, his forceful exhales simultaneously warming Mason and giving him chills.

Seconds later, Gray shifted again. His mouth was less than an inch from the tip of Mason's shaft.

He licked his lips, and Mason's cock jerked. He was desperate for contact with Gray, a touch, a kiss, anything. Gray blew on his cockhead, making a bead of pre-cum slide down his shaft. It tickled and tormented him.

Gray moved his head back and forth over Mason's thighs, so close Mason could almost feel the rasp of his stubble.

Every muscle in Mason's body was taut with need. "W-what are you doing?" he asked, the words breathless.

"Teasing you," Gray answered. He sat back on his heels and grinned.

"Please." The word escaped without Mason being able to stop it.

"You're not getting off that easily." Gray gave an evil laugh as he stood and stepped back, separating himself from Mason by a few feet. The big man undid his pants and pulled his cock out. Mason fucking loved that he hadn't been wearing anything under his form-fitting uniform pants.

Mason's balls drew up tight as he watched Gray lazily stroke himself. Cock ring or no, he was ready to shoot. All it would take was either man touching his cock. Hell, if they took the ring off, just watching the two of them might be enough.

"Suck me, Jack," Gray demanded. "Show him just how talented you are."

Jack fell to his knees in front of Gray. He wrapped one hand around the base of Gray's shaft and laid the other against the man's muscular thigh, steadying himself. As he took the tip of Gray's cock into his mouth, he looked over at Mason, holding his gaze as he swallowed more and more of Gray's enormous shaft.

Mason thought he might pass out watching Jack. Surely there couldn't be any more blood in his brain. His cock was red, his chest flushed. He was so hot he thought his blood might boil. He needed to be iced down, but he'd rather have Jack's mouth on his cock. Just one lick would be all it would take, and he'd combust. He wouldn't give a damn if he burned right up like a star in its last seconds of life as long as he got to feel Jack's gorgeous lips around his cock.

Jack took Gray all the way down, pressing his nose against the wiry hair at the base of his cock without gagging once. He bobbed his head, working Gray, making the big man groan and pant. He occasionally pulled off to lick and tease his slit or work his tongue around the edge of the head.

Mason grew more desperate every second. He tugged on his bonds, needing to get free, to join the two gorgeous men. He cursed the fucking cock ring. He was going to lose his mind if he didn't get some relief from the ache in his balls. Without the constriction, he could probably come just from watching Jack.

Jack swallowed Gray all the way again. His eyes sparkled with joy, making it obvious how much he loved what he was doing to his lover. He looked up at Gray, and when Gray looked down, his cold Dom mask slipped for a moment. He smiled at Jack, looking almost worshipful. Mason had never had anyone look at him like that. Jack grinned around Gray's shaft then began sucking in earnest, working his hand along the base and reaching his other hand deeper into Gray's pants.

Mason stared, openmouthed. He realized he was in danger of literally drooling on himself. He'd never seen anything so hot in his life.

Gray made a strangled sound and gripped Jack's head, thrusting into his mouth. Jack never faltered in his rhythm even though Gray fucked him relentlessly. Gray sank his teeth into his lower lip, but a rumbling groan rolled out anyway. He tensed and froze, shoving his cock even farther down Jack's throat. His whole body shook as he gave a hoarse shout and came.

Jack swallowed greedily as Gray shot into his mouth, but Gray's climax seemed endless, and despite how hard Jack worked, cum still escaped and ran down his chin. Gray pulled out and the last of his seed landed on Jack's face. Mason gasped. Jack looked fucking gorgeous covered in Gray's cum, kneeling, subservient, ready to take anything Gray wanted to give him.

Jack licked cum from his lower lip and Mason couldn't stop himself from begging. He was desperate to taste Gray against Jack's skin. "Please…let me."

Gray turned to him. "You want to clean him up, boy?"

It took Mason a few seconds to remember how to speak. "Y-yes, sir."

Gray grinned at Jack. "I do believe our prisoner really does want to co-operate."

Jack walked toward Mason on his knees. Mason leaned forward, tugging at his bonds, so turned on he thought he might lose his mind. He trembled with need, scared of how much he wanted these men. He swiped his tongue across Jack's lips, shuddering at the warm, musky taste of Gray.

Jack moaned and Mason licked him feverishly, running his tongue over Jack's chin, his cheeks, his lips. His cock ached as he reveled in cleaning Jack up. Knowing Gray was watching turned him on even more. He needed to please Gray, to please them both. He already knew he wanted to see them again. One night with them wouldn't be enough.

Jack tilted his head, exposing his neck, and Mason strained against his bonds, desperate to lick up every drop of Gray's cum off his partner. When he turned his attention back to Jack's lips, Jack opened for him and Mason pushed his tongue into the welcoming warmth. When Mason groaned, so did Gray.

"The two of you together are hotter than hell," Gray growled.

Mason pulled back and looked at him. Gray's eyes had darkened until they were almost black. His face was flushed, and Mason could see the flutter of his rapid pulse at his neck. He wanted to drag his teeth over it.

"Kiss him again," Gray ordered.

Mason was happy to oblige. While he explored every crevice of Jack's mouth, Gray knelt behind him and freed his arms. As soon as the bonds fell away, Mason took Jack's face in his hands and drove his tongue into Jack's mouth, fucking him with it the way he wanted Gray to fuck his ass.

Jack grabbed Mason's waist and tugged until he slid awkwardly off the chair and straddled Jack's lap. Jack wrapped his hand around Mason's cock, and Mason bucked up into the firm hold. The contact seared through him, burning him. The cock ring tightened around him like a vise. He whimpered against Jack's mouth. He had to come, had to get relief. Jack's fist pumped him faster and faster. His hand seemed to be alive with electric current that raced through Mason, sensitizing his entire body.

Suddenly Gray was behind him, the heat of his voice penetrated Mason's sexual fog.

"I'm going to spank you until your ass is as red as that straining cock of yours. Then if you beg nicely enough, I'll give you what you need." He ran his hand down Mason's back and traced the crease of his ass. Mason gasped against Jack's lips. Gray's hand was so hot, so big, so strong. Finally, this man he'd fantasized about for weeks was touching him, but it wasn't enough. He needed Gray to fuck, to possess him.

Mason pulled back from Jack a fraction of an inch. "Please." The word came out as an exhalation, but Gray heard him and laughed.

"So now you're hungry for what you wanted to deny us all."

"Didn't think you'd—"

"Damn right you didn't think. You should have offered your ass to me the first time we met."

Jack kissed him again, and Mason moaned into his mouth. Jack tightened his hold, digging his fingers into Mason's back then sliding down to cup his ass, rocking them together.

"When I've beaten your ass good and made you pay for making me wait, I'm going to fuck you hard and deep while you take Jack down your throat. You got that?"

Mason moaned. That was exactly what he wanted. Jack kissed him, holding his head in place and plundering his mouth.

"Let him go, Jack," Gray commanded.

Jack whimpered, working his hips, sliding their cocks together.

"Jack, are you asking for me to redden your ass too?"

Jack groaned but he released Mason and pushed him away.

Mason's cock throbbed, and he stared at Jack. The man's eyes were squeezed shut and his chest rose and fell rapidly. Jack looked pained, but he couldn't be as desperate to come as Mason. Mason wasn't sure he would even recover from being tormented like this. His balls ached so badly he thought they might burst.

Chapter Seven

When Jack opened his eyes, Mason saw lust and desperate need there. His cock was as red as Mason's and pre-cum beaded at the slit. Mason longed to taste it, but he didn't get the chance. With a snarl, Gray grabbed Mason's arm and jerked him to his feet. "We should never have started this here. How the hell am I going to get you two in bed?"

"I'll go anywhere. I just…." Mason hardly knew what he was saying. His brain had been deprived of blood for so long he didn't think it worked anymore.

Gray sighed as he caught Mason around the waist and hauled him over his shoulder in a fireman's carry.

"Jack, you better fucking follow us," he shouted as they started down the hall.

"Yes, sir." Jack's voice was strained. Mason raised his head so he could see him. Jack had his hand around his cock, working it, sliding his palm over the head with every firm upstroke. He sank his teeth into his lower lip. He was going to come any second, but Mason didn't want him to, not by himself, not from his own hand. Mason wanted his to be the one to bring him off. The thought of Jack driving deep into his mouth and shooting down his throat made him groan.

Gray whirled around then, making Mason swing wildly and thump against his back. Mason cried out as his aching cock brushed Gray's chest.

"Get up and start walking. You're not coming until he does," Gray commanded.

"Gray, please," Jack pleaded.

"No."

Mason heard what must have been Jack getting up, but he didn't dare shift to see, not when any movement might bring more friction to his cock. He'd never been this worked up, this tormented. He needed to come right that fucking second. Yet the thought of Gray's big strong hand cracking across his ass made him want to hold off, to see how much further the man could push him. What would it be like when they finally all came? He wasn't sure he would survive.

Gray turned around again, and Mason closed his eyes, fighting dizziness. With each of Gray's steps, Mason's cock slapped against Gray and a pathetic whimper escaped him. By the time Gray set him down, he was barely aware of his surroundings. Everything centered on the ache in his dick and his need for relief.

Gray slapped his ass, waking him partially from his lust-crazed stupor. "Bend over the bed, boy." He pushed Mason, forcing him to take a step toward the enormous bed that dominated the room. "Jack, hold his hands. We don't want him escaping his punishment."

Jack crawled up on the bed as Mason forced himself to obey. He lay over the end of the bed, grabbed hold of the covers, and stuck his ass out, careful not to move so close to the mattress that his cock brushed it. He was afraid that even the barest touch would make him come.

Jack took hold of his wrists and stretched his arms out straight as Gray laid a hand on his back. "Open your legs wider," Gray demanded. He pushed at Mason's ankles, encouraging him to widen his stance.

"Good. Do you think you can keep them apart or should I get a spreader bar?"

Gray's words shot straight to Mason's cock. The thought of his legs being held apart, restrained, so Gray could spank him, made him dizzy. He wanted to know how it would feel, but even more he wanted to please Gray, to be strong enough to take what Gray wanted to give. Gray was exactly what he'd fantasized about when he'd imagined submitting to a man, and yet, he was also more. Mason didn't want to disappoint him.

He jumped when Gray's hand cracked against his ass. "I expect an answer."

Mason turned his head so the mattress wouldn't muffle his words. "I can keep them apart. I…want…to…please you, sir." His breathing was so uneven he barely got the words out.

Gray caressed Mason's back. "Perfect. Somebody should have taken you in hand before now. You're so fucking gorgeous when you submit."

"God, yes," Jack said, caressing the inside of Mason's wrists with his thumbs. "I can't wait to see him writhing as you punish him."

"Do you remember your safeword?" Gray asked, his voice unsteady.

Mason shuddered at the realization that Gray was just as turned on as Mason and Jack were. "Yes, sir."

"And you will use it if you need to?"

"Yes, sir."

"Then get ready."

Jack's hands tightened around Mason's wrists, and Mason braced himself.

"Relax," Jack ordered him. "It hurts more if you're tense."

Mason tried to let go of some of the tension his body held but he couldn't, he was wound too tight. He drew in a breath, trying to prepare himself. Then Gray slapped his ass hard enough to force a grunt from him.

Crack! Gray's hand smacked Mason's other cheek.

Heat and pain bloomed over Mason's ass. He gasped for breath as Gray spanked him three more times in rapid succession. He writhed and cursed, fighting Jack's hold and stamping his feet.

Jack tugged on his arms, forcing him to keep his body stretched out on the bed.

Gray paused for several seconds, long enough for Mason to get himself under control, then he spanked the sorest part of Mason's ass, eliciting a yelp from him.

After that the blows came at random intervals, sometimes on the same spot, sometimes alternating side to side, and sometimes falling in an unpredictable pattern.

Mason nearly bit through his lip as he fought to hold himself together. Pain and need mingled inside him until he didn't know up from down. He shook with the intensity of what he felt, but eventually, he began to arch up, asking for more, meeting Gray's hand.

A storm was building inside him, and he was afraid of what would happen when it broke. He knew his ass was on fire, and yet he was cocooned somewhere, separate from sensation. He was whirling, soaring, and dipping, but he was terrified that he was going to fall when Gray stopped. He needed more, somehow more would help, if he could just....

Then the blows stopped coming. At first Mason thought Gray was just teasing him. He arched his back, begging silently for more. When he got no response, he whimpered, the sound embarrassing but impossible to stop.

Gray rubbed his hand over Mason's ass, touching the welts his fingers had raised. Mason sucked in his breath as he began to realize how very sore his ass was, but the pain was overridden by the throbbing of his cock.

"You've got to let go," Gray said.

"W-what do you mean?" Mason asked.

Jack shifted position and leaned down, bringing his mouth close to Mason's ear. "Give in to what you need. Sink into the pain, the need, and let go. Scream for us. Curse us. Release the tension that's threatening to tear you apart."

He understood then. The storm inside him. They wanted him to release it, but he was too scared. He would be exposed then. Whatever was happening between them no longer seemed like a game. It was something much more serious.

"Mason?" Gray's deep voice vibrated across his skin. Gray rubbed his back, and Jack kissed the top of his head.

"You can trust us," Jack whispered.

Gray caressed his sore ass with featherlight strokes. "You're so gorgeous like this. Let go and you'll get everything you need."

"So scared."

"I was too the first time he did this to me," Jack said. "But we're right here. We'll catch you."

Mason shivered but he pushed his ass out, begging again. His body knew what he needed.

Jack nipped at his ear. "We'll fuck you when we're done," he said. His hot breath and wicked words made Mason's cock jump despite his fear.

"Take some slow breaths," Gray said as he laid his hand on Mason's back. The comforting gesture allowed Mason to do what Gray asked. He drew air deep into his lungs and let it out slowly.

Gray bent and kissed him, right on the sorest place on his ass. The kiss was soft, tender, and Mason knew he was going to give Gray everything he wanted, no matter how scared he was of his feelings for these two men.

"You ready?" Gray asked, his voice low and soothing.

"Yes, sir."

Gray slapped his ass, the sound reverberating in the room.

Jack drew in a sharp breath. "This is so fucking hot."

Mason arched his back, desperate for more.

Gray gave it to him, spanking him over and over. Mason's groans grew louder until he was crying out, cursing, screaming, begging, letting the storm loose so it could batter at all of them.

"Three more," Gray warned him. The last blow was harder than any that had come before it. Mason screamed. Gray reached around and unsnapped the cock ring. A ball of fire rolled down his spine and exploded. Heat and light and pleasure so sharp it seemed to cut him in two pulsed through and around him as he shot his load in powerful bursts. When he was wrung dry, he slumped against the bed, panting.

Jack let him go and rubbed his wrists. Mason realized they were sore from being held for so long. He must have really been fighting Jack's hold at the end, but he only vaguely remembered what he'd done as he'd sunk into submission.

Jack slid closer, and Mason opened his eyes to look at him. His cock was close to Mason's face, thick and red and wet with pre-cum. Mason licked his lips and swallowed as he tried to raise up on his elbows. He needed a taste. But he slipped and fell back onto the mattress, even that small effort was too much for his exhausted body. Jack stroked his head. "Just relax for now."

He lay against the soft bed, trying to remember to breathe. He heard tearing and realized it was the sound of Gray opening a condom. Was Gray really going to fuck him? He wanted it so bad, but when

Gray thrust against the sore flesh of his ass, it was going to hurt like hell.

A few seconds later, Gray pressed his finger, cool and slick with lube, against Mason's entrance. He circled Mason's pucker, teasing the sensitive flesh until Mason moaned and pushed back against him. He slid in slowly.

Mason's cock started to swell again though he would have thought that impossible this soon after he'd nearly come apart. He squirmed, trying to force Gray deeper, but Gray pulled out and added a second finger. Gray eased his digits in and out until Mason thought he would go insane if Gray didn't pick up the pace. He wiggled his hips, pushing back and fucking himself on Gray's fingers. The tension that had poured out of him while Gray slapped his ass started to rise again. "Fuck me, sir. Please," he begged.

"Are you sorry for teasing us?" Gray asked, his voice hard.

Mason whimpered. "Yes, God yes. If I'd known—"

"Do you promise to tell us exactly what you want from now on?"

"Yes, sir, please!" The words became a cry as Gray's fingers curled against his prostate.

Gray pulled his fingers from Mason's ass. Mason groaned at the loss, but he heard the sound of Gray's hand sliding back and forth, slicking his cock.

Gray spread Mason's ass cheeks, letting his fingers dig into Mason's sore flesh. Mason bit his lip to keep from cursing him, but he didn't really care about the pain. He'd suffer anything to be impaled on Gray's cock right that fucking second.

Gray positioned himself and surged forward. Mason made a strangled sound. He'd never been so full. It was too much and not enough. He tried to push back and take Gray deeper, but Gray held his hips, making him wait. When Gray had given him time to adjust to the invasion of his fat cock and he'd started to relax, his lover pushed in deeper, slow and steady at first then ramming himself in the last bit so his body smacked against Mason's.

"Fuck!" Mason cried.

Jack grabbed his hand and squeezed. "His cock feels so good inside you, doesn't it?"

"Yes, oh God, yes."

Gray pulled back then pushed forward again, moving more slowly than Mason wanted him to. "Harder," he demanded.

Gray growled. "Suck Jack and I'll give you what you need."

Mason raised up, finding the ability to support himself this time. He reached for Jack's shaft, and Jack positioned himself so Mason could swallow him down. When he started sucking Jack in earnest, Gray started fucking him like he wanted, hard and fast with no mercy.

Seconds later, Gray changed his angle and slid over Mason's prostate. Mason nearly choked himself on Jack's cock as sensation zinged through him. Gray kept hammering into him, hitting his sweet spot again and again. The dizzying pleasure combined with the sensation of Jack's dick filling his mouth drove Mason to the edge of insanity.

He went wild, driving back onto Gray while taking Jack all the way down, milking his cock, tugging on his balls, determined to make him shoot so hard he'd scream. Mason hummed around Jack as Gray pounded into him, used him, owned him. Then Gray fisted Mason's cock, pumping him with firm, sure strokes. Mason lost it.

He pulled off Jack and cried out. His body bowed. His thighs tensed, rock hard. He cursed and yelled and struggled for breath. Gray kept banging him, digging his fingers into Mason's hips so hard he'd surely have bruises.

Then Gray gave a strangled shout, rammed into Mason, and came with short, ferocious jerks of his hips.

Mason took Jack back into his mouth as he enjoyed Gray's shudders of pleasure. In seconds, Jack was coming too, shooting his musky cum down Mason's throat. Mason took it all, swallowing again and again.

When Jack softened Mason let him go, and the three of them collapsed together. Gray tugged on Mason's waist until he pulled both of them up onto the bed. Mason drifted into unconsciousness, more sated than he'd ever been.

Mason woke up some time later when Gray stirred beside him. The big man was curled around his back, and he had his leg hooked over Jack's prone form. Gray groaned and shifted, making the springs of the bed creak. "Fuck, I never even got undressed," he groaned.

Mason rose up on his elbows and looked over at Gray, blinking the sleep out of his eyes. Gray's uniform shirt still covered his chest. It was rumpled and had suspicious stains along the hem. His pants were tangled around his knees. The sight made Mason smile. It also stirred his cock. He was already thinking about how much he'd like to be "arrested" again.

Gray must have guessed the direction of his thoughts. "We need sleep first."

Mason nodded, only a little disappointed, because he knew Gray was right. After watching Gray kick off his pants and drop them on the floor, Mason forced himself to sit up. He winced at how sore his ass was, but he moved cautiously to the edge of the bed and lowered one foot to the floor.

"What are you doing?"

He looked at Gray. The man's eyes were narrowed like he was about to accuse Mason of another crime. "I was…uh…going to get dressed and go. You said you needed to sleep."

"I do need to sleep, curled up with you and Jack."

Gray said the words in his loud, booming voice, and Jack stirred.

"What's wrong?" he asked, squinting up at them.

"Mason was about to run, and I told him he needs to stay."

Jack rolled his eyes. "How about asking instead? Playtime is over."

Gray harrumphed.

Jack reached for Mason and laid a hand on his arm. "Please stay."

Mason looked from one man to the other.

Gray reached for his hand. "I'd like you to stay."

Mason saw uncertainty in the strong man's eyes. Was this more than just a fun fuck for him too? He glanced at Jack, who was looking at his partner with unmistakable love on his face. That look shattered Mason's confidence. They were a couple. He shouldn't intrude. The three of them had fun together. That should be enough.

"I don't think…."

Gray ran a hand through his hair. "Look, I'm not good with words."

Jack snorted.

"Shut up, asshole."

Jack laughed. "He's good with other things."

Mason couldn't help but grin. The two of them arguing while Gray wore his uniform shirt and nothing else was adorable and sexy as hell all at once.

"This may have seemed casual and fast, but we don't do this a lot. We've played around with someone else a few times, but with you…." Gray shrugged. "I don't know, it's not just—would you just stay the night? Please?"

Mason's heart pounded.

Jack grinned. "He's trying to say that we really like you, and we don't want to send you off like some trick. This was meant to be more than that, and we want to snuggle up with you now."

Gray nodded. "Yeah, what he said."

Mason knew better. He could so easily fall for them, and that would lead to him getting hurt. They wanted more than a quick fuck, but they were still a couple, and he was still going to walk away alone whether it was now or days or weeks from now. Even knowing that, he couldn't resist their earnest expressions and their obviously sincere desire for him to stay. So when Jack lifted the covers and motioned from him to crawl back under them, he did, and he slept better than he had in months.

Chapter Eight

When the alarm went off the next morning, Jack got up first. He took his turn in the shower then headed out of the room, mumbling something about coffee and breakfast. Once he was gone, Mason forced himself to leave the warm cocoon of their bed. Gray made a few growly protests as Mason extracted himself from the man's arms, but he didn't fully wake.

Mason took longer than he should have in the shower, letting the hot water pound away some of the soreness from the night's exertions. As he enjoyed the soothing heat, he wondered if Gray and Jack would ask him back again. He wanted them to, and yet he didn't. He was already much too attached to them. He craved the feel of their hands on him, the taste of their skin, the slap of Gray's hand on his ass, and the burning stretch of Gray filling him up. He wanted Jack to fuck him, as well. His cock swelled, and his hand dropped to it as he imagined them both fucking him at the same time, something he'd never done.

He forced himself to ignore the powerful fantasy. He needed to get dressed and go home, not stand in their shower jacking off. He shouldn't have stayed in the first place. No matter how much he wanted them, it would be better if he treated this like a one-time thing. He wondered if he'd be able to slip out the door and run without having to face them. Was he really that much of a coward? No, but he was that scared, because he longed for more than just another round in their bed. He wanted to get to know them. He wanted a relationship with them, but three-ways made for hot sex, not long-term partnerships. It was difficult enough to make things work with one other person, balancing three people's needs had to be next to impossible. Besides, Gray and Jack were happy together. He wouldn't fuck with that.

Gray stirred when Mason got out of the shower. He rolled out of bed and grunted something that might have been a greeting or might have simply been an attempt to get Mason to move out of his way so he could get to the en suite bathroom. Mason couldn't help staring at his fine ass as he walked away, but once Gray had shut the bathroom door, he dressed and headed for the kitchen, seduced by the smell of coffee. As much as he would prefer to sneak away, he couldn't leave without saying something to Jack. He intended to thank him for a wonderful night, grab a quick cup of coffee, and get out of there.

When he saw Jack behind the counter stirring a bowl of batter, he was transfixed. When he was in his police uniform, exuding confidence, Mason found Jack sexy as hell. Here in his kitchen, hair wet from the shower, wearing an old t-shirt and scruffy jeans, relaxed and so focused on cooking that he hadn't heard Mason come in, he was stunning.

Mason swallowed, trying to moisten his suddenly dry mouth. He didn't move, scared he'd disturb the scene in front of him. He guessed that Jack was making waffles since he had a waffle iron out on the counter. Mason hadn't had a homemade waffle since he used to spend occasional nights with his grandma when he was a kid.

Jack laid down the fork he'd been stirring with and reached a finger into the bowl. When he brought it to his lips and licked the batter off, Mason bit his lip to keep from moaning. He wanted to reach into the bowl for more batter and paint Jack with it, then slowly, carefully lick it off. He couldn't help thinking about licking Jack's face clean after he'd sucked Gray off the night before. Heat raced to his cheeks as fast as it was going to his cock. Had he really done that?

Jack noticed Mason as he opened the waffle iron and started to pour the batter over the surface. "Good morning. Did you sleep well?"

Mason's heart pounded and panic threatened to consume him. What was he doing here in the midst of this domestic scene? He needed to leave. Fast. "Um, yeah, but I should really get going."

Jack frowned. "But I'm making breakfast for you."

Several seconds passed before Mason found his voice. Talking to Jack now in the kitchen was scarier than submitting to him and Gray could ever be.

"There better be some for me too," Gray hollered as he walked into the kitchen. Mason turned to look at him. He was fresh from the shower, and his wet hair was curling up at the ends. He wore low-slung sweats and a dark green t-shirt that strained across his shoulders.

A vivid memory of Gray squeezing Mason's hips as he drove into him with hard, punishing strokes made Mason momentarily dizzy.

He shouldn't stay another second. He could not let himself get pulled further into their world. He'd had some great sex, but that was all it could be. Jack and Gray's love showed in the tender looks they gave each other, the way they touched, the way they knew what the other was thinking.

Mason believed that they considered him a friend and not just a quick fuck. They wouldn't have asked him to stay the night otherwise, and Jack certainly wouldn't be making waffles for a hookup. He wished he could be happy being friends with benefits, but as it was, his desire for them was bordering on obsession. If he stayed there, in their house, watching how easy they were with each other, he'd only become more enthralled and more desperate for something he couldn't have.

Jack grinned at Gray, oblivious to Mason's discomfort. "I tripled the recipe just for you."

Mason glanced at the bowl. It looked like Jack had enough batter to make waffles for the whole police force.

"Thank you, but I really should go." Mason's voice was embarrassingly shaky.

"You're not leaving without breakfast." Gray took his arm and tugged him toward the kitchen.

Jack rolled his eyes as he ripped open a package of bacon and started laying pieces in a frying pan. "Stop being a Neanderthal. You can't just order Mason around."

"Everyone would do better to just listen to me, you included."

Mason got the impression that Gray was referring to something specific, but Jack blew Gray off. He looked back at Mason from where he stood at the sink, washing his hands. "We really would like you to stay."

"I…um…I've got to get some errands done before I head to work."

Gray glared at him, and Mason was sure Gray knew he was lying. But instead of calling him out, he positioned himself behind Jack, who was once again in front of the waffle maker. With his gaze still on Mason, Gray wrapped his arms around Jack and reached down, cupping his lover's cock. "I was hoping we could go another round or two once Jack got us energized."

Mason sucked in his breath as Gray stroked Jack through his pants. Jack pushed back into him, sliding his ass against Gray's crotch without losing his concentration on making waffles and turning the bacon.

Staying would be so easy, good food, hot sex, two men he was falling in love with. *What the fuck?* No! He wasn't in love with them, couldn't be in love with them.

Jack finished pouring batter and closed the lid of the waffle iron. He turned his head so he could kiss Gray, his expression pure bliss. The thought of a man looking at him like that made Mason's chest ache.

"That would be…um…great, but I should really go."

"Are you okay?" Gray asked. "Did I freak you out last night? Things don't usually get that intense so quickly."

Intense didn't begin to describe it, but Mason shook his head. "No. I loved what you did to me, all of it. It's not that. I just can't stay."

Mason could tell that they wanted to keep questioning him. Both of them were far too perceptive not to pick up on his unease, but he wasn't about to tell them that he was falling for them or that he was jealous of what they had with each other. They deserved their happiness, and he needed to walk away.

*****

Mason unlocked the door of his tiny garage apartment. It was far from luxurious, but it was clean and in good repair, and he was close enough to Duke's east campus that he could take his daily jog around the perimeter wall and pretend he was still a student.

He put the plastic container of waffles and bacon that Jack had packed for him on the counter and opened his utensil drawer in search of a fork, still in awe of Jack's skills in the kitchen. If Jack and Gray had stayed at his place, they would have been lucky to get cereal or toast. His idea of cooking was boiling pasta and opening a jar of sauce or heating up a frozen pizza.

How awesome would it be to wake up to a meal made by Jack every morning? Of course, he probably didn't make a big breakfast on days when he and Gray had to work, but even coffee and toast shared with Jack and Gray would be better than anything he might have alone.

Mason didn't do the errands he was supposed to do that afternoon. Instead, he spent the day lying on the couch—on his side thanks to his sore ass, which reminded him of Jack and Gray every time he moved—feeling sorry for himself and watching sad movies.

Jack called just before Mason headed to work that evening, but Mason let the call go to voice mail. He could feel his brain freezing up at the very thought of talking to Jack. What would he say? They'd given him an amazing night, and he practically ran from their house like it was on fire.

During his first break at work, Mason sent Jack a quick text. He still wasn't ready to hear Jack's sexy voice. When he thought about the things Jack had said to him and the way it felt to be caught between him and Gray, heat filled his face. He really hoped they wouldn't come into the bar that night. He'd have to face them eventually, but he wasn't ready. He wasn't sure he'd ever be over the intensity of the emotions they'd made him feel.

He'd told them he wasn't freaked out by what they'd done, but he wasn't being completely honest. He'd never come that close to a total meltdown, and he'd never surrendered to anyone so utterly. It was as if Gray and Jack had reached inside his mind, pulled out his most secret fantasies, and then gone a step further and discovered things Mason didn't even know he longed for. They'd made him feel accepted and cared for in a way no one ever had. He'd never be able to explain to anyone how being tied up and spanked made him feel cherished, but it did.

Gray may have dominated him, and Jack may have been his willing accomplice, but Gray had also worshipped him and taken the time to give him what he needed in a way no other man had even come close to doing. And Jack knew just when Mason started getting tense or scared. He knew the right words to say to calm him down and give him permission to simply enjoy what he felt. Mason had been safe with them, as he'd known he would be. How had he gotten so lucky to find such caring lovers, and so unlucky to feel more for them than he should?

Mason tried to put them out of his mind as he worked, but the more he tried not to think of them, the more he thought of nothing else. Nothing but Gray looming over him while he was tied to the chair, almost but not quite touching him, making him want to beg. Nothing but the sound of Gray's hand slapping his ass and the bite of erotic pain that made him want to scream. Nothing but letting go of everything—tension, self-control, any attempt to hide how deeply he felt for them. All of it stirred Mason up, making him crazy, making him want to call them and ask to do it all again.

Gray had used the words "next time", but Mason shouldn't sleep with them again even if they did ask, because while most of his memories made him horny as hell, he also remembered the way Jack and Gray looked at each other. They hid their feelings for one another well enough in the bar, only someone who already knew would see it, but at home the depth of those feelings were more than obvious.

Mason squeezed his eyes shut. The memories of hot sex he could handle, but the rest, the agonizing emotions Gray dragged from him, the sweetness of their concern for him, Jack's insistence on sending him home with a hot breakfast, those were the things that would do him in, make him feel too much, make him not want to let things end, ever.

A few minutes later, Mason's phone buzzed in his pocket. He pulled it out and saw a text from Jack.

Are you free tomorrow night? Want to meet at our place for dinner?

Dinner at their place? More of Jack's cooking? For the sake of his sanity, he should say no. He could easily pretend he had plans or that he had to work. His fingers hovered over the keypad. Then, before he could stop himself, he responded.

What time and what should I bring?

Chapter Nine

The next evening, Mason picked up some wine and took the bus to Gray and Jack's house. When he raised his hand to knock, he realized it was shaking. Why did he have to make such a big deal out of this? He was going to have a home-cooked dinner and then get fucked by two hot guys, two hot cops even. He should be excited, not scared.

Gray opened the door and Mason's eyes widened at the sight of him. No matter how many times he saw the man, he never stopped being surprised by his sheer size. That night he was wearing a t-shirt that said "Badass Cop", which made Mason smile.

"You gonna come in?" Gray asked, chuckling.

Mason realized he'd been staring for quite some time, something that always seemed to happen around Gray.

"Yeah. Sorry."

"I don't mind at all," Gray said. His low voice was so fucking sexy. Mason wondered if he could come just from listening to him.

As Mason walked into the house, he let his gaze roam Gray's body some more. He sucked in his breath when he saw Gray's cock, hard and straining against the thinning fabric of his worn jeans.

Mason wanted to fall to his knees, unzip Gray's pants, and take Gray into his mouth right that second. Probably bad etiquette though. Dinner first, then blowjobs. Wasn't that how a date worked?

Why the hell were they pretending this was a date anyway? Jack and Gray wanted to fuck him, and it wasn't like they had to try and seduce him. Why else would they—

"Mason," Jack called, interrupting his thoughts.

"Hi! Um…thanks for inviting me." Mason suddenly realized he'd never really greeted Gray.

He turned and looked at him over his shoulder. "I'm really sorry. I didn't even say hello."

Gray chuckled. "Don't worry. Your look said it all." Gray laid one of his big, warm hands against the small of Mason's back and guided him toward Jack.

Whatever Jack was cooking smelled heavenly, earthy and rich and garlicky, definitely Italian. Jack let his gaze sweep up and down Mason's body. Mason's cock had already taken a serious interest in Gray, and now it filled more as Jack looked at him like he was going to be dinner.

"I brought wine." He lifted up the grocery bag he'd been holding, and Gray grabbed it and set it on the counter.

Jack wiped his hands on a towel and came around from behind the kitchen island. He pulled Mason into his arms and kissed him, not a chaste greeting kiss, but a kiss filled with all the passion Mason was trying to keep bottled up. Maybe blowjobs and other fun didn't have to wait until they'd eaten after all.

As he and Jack explored each other's mouths with leisurely abandon, Gray stepped behind him, grabbed onto his hips, and pulled him back, fitting his erection between Mason's cheeks. He kissed and nibbled Mason's neck, making him moan into Jack's mouth.

A few seconds later, Jack released him and used his grip on Mason's shoulders to turn him to face Gray.

Gray cupped Mason's face and licked at his lips before kissing him, tenderly, reverently at first and then harder until they were devouring each other. Jack ground himself against Mason's ass, muttering compliments about how hot Mason was.

Finally Gray pulled away and grinned.

Mason swayed and Jack steadied him. "You ok?"

He nodded and then shook his head and laughed. "I don't know. I think so."

He turned around and Jack gave him an assessing look. "We need to feed him or he's going to pass out."

"No, I—"

"Yes," Gray agreed. "Dinner first."

"Are you sure?" Mason hoped he didn't sound too whiny.

Gray smiled. "Anticipation is good for you, remember?"

"Please tell me you aren't going to send me home and make me wait again."

Gray raised a brow. "Are you going to complain if I do?" His tone was dark, the same one he'd used when pretending to be the bad cop.

Mason shuddered. "No, sir."

"Good." He ran his hand up and down Mason's back. "I have another surprise for you."

Mason suddenly felt dizzy.

Gray looked at Jack. "Is dinner ready yet?"

A laugh burst from Jack. "Who's impatient now?"

"I'm just hungry, damn it," Gray growled.

"Sure you are." Jack laughed.

Mason watched the two men banter with each other and a deep longing to be a part of what they had hit him again. Where was he going to find another man who could dominate him like Gray or make him smile like Jack? And how the hell was he going to give them up when the time came?

Gray opened a bottle of wine and poured each of them a glass while Jack served dinner: baked ziti, crusty garlic bread dripping with butter, and a simple green salad with a homemade Italian dressing. After tasting everything, Mason looked at Jack, amazed. "This is incredible. Where did you learn to cook like this?"

Jack gave an uncharacteristically shy smile. "My mom mostly, but I also watched a lot of cooking shows after I left home. I was used to really good food, and I couldn't live off frozen shit like the other guys at the academy. After I met Gray, I had someone to cook for so I just kept practicing."

"And I am very appreciative," Gray said, making the words sound dirty. Mason could imagine just how he expressed his appreciation.

Jack actually blushed, letting Mason know that Gray's efforts to get Jack to keep cooking for him must have been extraordinary.

"Well, I can't cook for shit, but I can clean and I make good cocktails," Mason said, then immediately regretted his words. He sounded like he was trying to sell himself. They didn't need his paltry skills. Not when they had each other.

Gray smirked. "We know exactly what you can do."

Mason resisted the urge to fan himself.

Gray turned to Jack. "What do you think? Should we save dessert for later?"

Jack raised a brow. "I thought Mason was dessert."

Mason swallowed hard as Jack looked him up and down.

Gray licked his lips. "He sure will taste good, but I know you made something for us so don't try to deny it. You're not going to leave me and Mason in bed at two AM and sneak down to eat it all yourself."

At least Mason wasn't going to be forced to anticipate for too long if Gray was planning for him to spend the night in their bed.

Another night with them. Another chance to snuggle in bed and let them seep further under his skin.

"I need to go to the bathroom," Mason blurted out. Suddenly, he was desperate for a few moments alone.

"Are you ok?" Jack looked concerned.

"Yeah, I'm fine. I just drank my wine too fast."

Fitting In

Jack looked over his shoulder at Gray. What were they saying with that silent communication thing couples could do? Did they think they'd scared him? He wanted to reassure them, but he was scared, just probably not for the reasons they thought.

He rose on unsteady legs and took a step. Gray grabbed his arm. "Tell me the truth."

What could he say? That he longed to be looked at the way they looked at each other? That he was afraid of what he was feeling because it was way more than lust? That he thought he might lose his mind over them?

"It's just…a lot. All this." He gestured around stupidly as if the room was too much: the bright walls, the antique table, the limited but pleasant decor, the mouth-watering dessert Jack had taken from the fridge and placed on the counter.

Jack touched his arm and looked in the same direction. "It's only tiramisu. It looks complex, but it's very easy to assemble."

Mason was sure he was talking about more than delicious dessert, but he chose not to comment on the deeper meaning. "I love tiramisu."

"Then you'll be fine. Just relax and enjoy."

"I'll try." Jack was a good man and so was Gray. Gray might not know how to express himself as well as Jack, but they were a good team. No wonder they'd been partnered on the force. It sucked that they had to stay in the closet to keep working together.

"Good. I'll serve us some dessert while you use the bathroom," Jack said.

Mason relieved himself, drank some water, and messed around with his hair for a few minutes. Then he took a slow, deep breath and forced himself to go back to the kitchen.

"Better now?" Jack asked.

Mason nodded. And he was, a little.

"Good, then let's get on with dessert," Gray said.

"Which one?" Jack asked, an impish grin on his face.

Gray raised his brow and stared him down.

Suddenly, Mason wasn't sure if he was okay or not. He wanted this, wanted them, but Gray was too intense. He forced more emotion out of Mason than Mason would've thought possible, and Jack was like sensuality personified. Together…. He shivered.

"I think he's a little nervous," Jack said.

"Then help him get over it." Gray grinned. "Slip the dessert plates in the fridge and then work on settling him down while I get things ready."

Things? What things? What is he planning?

Jack dealt with the tiramisu, and Gray walked over to Mason and laid his hand against the back of Mason's neck. That gesture was possessive and controlling and both comforting and unsettling at the same time. He slid his hand up into Mason's hair and rubbed Mason's scalp with his thumb. "You're going to love this."

He bent and kissed the top of his head in an oddly sweet gesture. Then he walked away without looking back.

Jack cupped Mason's chin, forcing him to turn and look Jack in the eyes.

"He's right. You'll love what he has planned for you, but please let us know if you need to slow down or if it's too much right now."

"I will." Mason whispered the words as Jack leaned in, bringing their lips together. The kiss started off gentle. Then Jack increased the pressure. Mason forced himself to stay still and let him set the pace.

Jack walked him backward until he bumped into a stool. He sat and opened his legs. Jack pushed between them, and Mason took hold of his waist. He dropped his head back, and Jack held onto the sides of his face and plundered his mouth. When they both needed air, Jack let him go.

"Hold onto the stool," he ordered.

Reluctantly, Mason took his hands off Jack's waist and gripped the seat of the stool.

Jack crowded closer, forcing Mason's legs wider. Hot need pulsed through Mason when Jack pushed a hand between them and rubbed Mason's stiff cock.

"Mmm," Jack moaned into Mason's mouth. "So fucking hard for us. So ready."

Mason nodded frantically. "Please."

Jack let him go and knelt. "Don't move."

Mason didn't even breathe.

Jack grinned as he unfastened Mason's pants and freed his erection.

Mason squeezed the sides of the stool so hard he thought it might crack. But he didn't move. He wasn't about to do anything to stop Jack from using his mouth on him. Jack gripped his shaft and licked the tip, closing his eyes and savoring the drop of pre-cum he'd captured on his tongue. He looked up at Mason, his blue eyes darkened with lust. Holding Mason's gaze, he took just the tip into his mouth, sucking much too gently for what Mason needed. Then he started working the underside with his tongue, pressing, sliding, teasing. Mason panted, desperate to force Jack farther onto his shaft.

Without warning, Jack stopped and stood. "That's enough for now. We should go find Gray."

Mason stared openmouthed. "But—"

"Gray said to get you comfortable. If I do more, he'll take it out on both of us. We don't want that, do we?"

"Yes. No. Fuck."

Jack smiled. "This is going to be so good."

Mason realized he was still gripping the chair. His hands ached when he pulled them away. Jack took one and then the other, massaging them until they felt better. Then he tugged and pulled Mason to standing. Mason followed in a daze, holding one of Jack's hands and not bothering to refasten his pants. He doubted Gray would want him clothed.

Chapter Ten

Instead of leading Mason to Gray and Jack's bedroom, Jack headed into the spare room. Where Mason had seen a treadmill before, Gray had placed something else. At first, Mason thought it was a weight bench, but then he looked closer and heat filled his face. "Is that a…um…"

Jack laughed. "A spanking bench? Why yes, it is."

Mason stared at the low, leather-covered bench, the straps dangling from each of the corners ending in cuffs lined with something that looked soft and cushioning.

Gray laid a warm hand on his back. "Try it out. Just lay over it and see how it feels. If you want to stay we'll see what you think of the cuffs, if not, we'll go to the bedroom." His voice was low and encouraging.

Mason's heart pounded, but he knew he wanted this. He wanted to see how it would feel to be strapped to the bench while Gray reddened his ass. He started to take off his shirt because he wanted to feel the leather against his naked skin, but after undoing two buttons he froze and looked back at Gray. "May I strip?"

Gray smiled, and Mason felt a wave of pride wash over him. He'd pleased his lover.

"You may," Gray said, then he looked at Jack. "I want you naked too."

Mason shucked his clothes and shoes as quickly as he could, hoping Gray hadn't expected him to make it a sexy strip show. He didn't think he was capable of that as nervous as he was.

He positioned himself on the bench. The pad where he knelt was soft and supportive under his knees. He could stay there a long time and not be sore. He lay over the smooth, cool leather and resisted the urge to rub himself on it. He tried to relax, letting his arms drop and brush the floor, hoping he could work up the courage to ask Gray to strap him in.

Jack finished undressing then stepped up beside Mason and rubbed his back with long strokes that almost reached his ass. After a few seconds, Mason was arching up, silently asking for more contact, but Jack didn't give him what he needed. Instead, he picked up one of the cuffs and brushed it across Mason's arm. "You ready?"

Mason took a slow breath. He was scared, but he wanted to try it. "Yes."

Jack moved back, and Gray reached for the cuff, taking Mason's wrist in his other hand. "Use your safeword if you need to. Don't hesitate."

Mason looked up at him and nodded.

Gray arched his brow.

"Yes, sir." Mason's voice was steadier than he expected it to be.

Gray closed the cuff around Mason's wrist. Then he strapped in Mason's other arm while Jack secured his ankles.

Mason wiggled, testing the bonds. They held him tight against the bench. He wasn't going to be able to escape from anything Gray wanted to give him. His breaths came short and shallow as panic started to set in.

Gray laid a big hand on his back, and Jack knelt by his head.

"It's okay," Jack said, pushing Mason's hair off his face. "Breathe deep with me."

Mason tried to match his inhalations with Jack's, but his instinct to fight was strong.

Gray caressed his ass with slow circles. "You're so beautiful like this. I want to watch you struggle while I work your ass over. I want to know you can't escape me."

Mason drew in a shuddering breath. "Want that too. Want to…surrender."

"Good."

The word was low and filled with promise, and somehow, it soothed Mason's nerves. His panic fled, replaced by need.

Gray rubbed his ass firmly with both hands, warming it up. Then he slid the fingers of one hand along Mason's crease and teased his hole before dipping lower and toying with his balls.

Mason arched into Gray's touch as much as the cuffs would allow. "Need you," he pleaded.

"What do you need?" Gray asked, his voice gravelly.

Mason's mind was too scattered to form a coherent thought. What did he need? He wanted to surrender, to let go the way he had before, to please

Gray. He wanted Gray to make his ass burn then to fuck him into oblivion. "Can't. Think."

Gray slapped his ass. The sting jolted Mason back to reality.

"Is that what you want?" Gray asked.

Mason tried to remember how to speak.

Gray spanked his other cheek. "Tell me."

"Y-yes. That and more."

"Don't hold back. I want to hear you scream."

"Yes, sir."

Gray spanked him harder. His ass was on fire, yet it wasn't enough. He needed…. *Fuck!* He didn't know what he needed. His cock was so hard. Gray smacked him again and again. The pain made him feel so alive, safe, cared for. What the fuck did that mean? How could pain be comforting?

Gray stopped. He caressed Mason's abused flesh. Mason became aware again of Jack, still there, stroking his shoulder, kissing his head. Jack's cock strained upward. He looked as painfully hard as Mason felt.

Gray knelt beside Jack. Mason looked at him, his gaze dropping to Gray's hands. He held a crop like the one Mason's sister used when riding horses.

"I'd like to use this on you."

Mason stared, trying to catch his breath, trying to think.

"Are you okay with that?" Gray asked.

It would sting much worse than Gray's hand. "H-how bad does it hurt?"

Jack squeezed his hand. "It's a more intense spanking, but it's so good, and Gray will know how much you can take."

91

Gray nodded. "I'll go slowly, and even if you want me to, I won't work you too hard, not today."

"Please," Mason begged, hardly aware of what he was asking for.

"Please what?"

"Please, sir."

Gray glared at him. "Tell me exactly what you want."

"Please use the crop, sir."

Gray smiled. "Much better."

He rose and stepped behind Mason again. "Hold his hand," Gray commanded Jack.

Jack did. And Mason squeezed him tight.

Gray rubbed Mason's ass with the crop and then brought it down against the sore flesh.

Mason cried out, the sting shocking him.

"That's good," Gray said. "Let it out."

Gray cracked the crop across his ass again.

"Fuck!" Mason squeezed Jack's hand so hard he thought he might break Jack's fingers.

"I'm going to give you three more. Do not hold back."

Mason felt like he was floating. Only Jack anchored him to the room, even the bonds seemed unreal.

Jack tried to pull away.

"No!" Mason yelled.

"Okay, I'm here," Jack reassured him. "I just don't want to keep you from letting go."

Mason shook his head. "Need you both."

"Stay with him, Jack," Gray commanded.

"Yes, sir."

Gray cropped him three more times in rapid succession. He screamed with the last blow and realized tears were running down his face. What the hell was wrong with him?

Gray and Jack worked together to free him, but he was barely aware of what they were doing.

Jack pulled him onto his lap, and Mason straddled him clumsily, their cocks brushing each other. Gray pushed on his back, tumbling them over onto the floor. He slid a spit-slick finger into Mason as Mason worked himself against Jack.

Jack took Mason's face in his hands and pulled him down for a fierce kiss. "So gorgeous, so amazing. Want you," Jack muttered against his lips.

Mason nodded frantically. He wasn't capable of talking or even thinking. All he knew was his desperate need to have both of these men.

Gray added another finger, opening him up. His ass cheeks burned as if Gray had set fire to them, and yet Gray's finger-fucking felt so good. "Inside me, please."

Gray petted him with one hand while he pushed his fingers slowly in and out. Mason pushed back, trying to take him deeper.

"Don't want to hurt you." That seemed a strange statement after he'd just cropped Mason's ass, but Mason understood. That pain was different than taking his ass too fast, too hard, but Mason didn't want to wait another second.

"Want it. Don't care if it hurts."

"Fuck. Mason, I…" Gray rubbed a hand over the hot flesh of his ass. "So red, so…"

"Good. So fucking good. Please!"

Jack groaned, grabbing Mason around the waist and bucking up against him. Their pre-cum eased the slide of their cocks against each other.

Gray stood long enough to strip, then he covered his cock with a condom and pushed into Mason. Suddenly, that thick shaft was all Mason could think about. Gray moved slowly, stretching Mason, making him claw at Jack. He fought to relax and take Gray deeper, but he was losing his mind.

Gray laid a hand on Mason's back, holding him down, pushing him into Jack so Jack couldn't more easily work himself against Mason.

Mason whimpered. "Need you. Damn it, Gray."

Gray growled. "You'll wait."

Jack dug his fingers into Mason and humped up against him furiously. Mason kissed him, trying to pour all his need into Jack.

Gray pushed deeper, then his hips brushed Mason's burning ass. Mason would have cried out if his mouth hadn't been fused to Jack's.

Gray pulled out slowly then drove in harder. Mason fought him. He was too full. His ass ached. He needed…he needed….

"Breathe," Gray ordered.

Mason tried.

Jack tightened his hold on Mason as panic threatened again. He didn't really want to stop but he was terrified by how Gray and Jack overwhelmed him, made him feel too much.

Jack nibbled on his neck. "Relax," he whispered. Mason tried to, but he couldn't.

"Gray!" Mason cried out as Gray shifted his angle, causing his cock to brush Mason's prostate.

"Better?" Gray asked.

Mason nodded.

Jack licked and sucked his neck. Gray waited until Mason was begging with his body again, apprehension fading in a swirl of lust. "Ready?" Gray asked.

"Yes." He forced out the single, strangled word as Jack reached between them and pumped his cock.

Mason was possessed, caught between them, and it was both the best and the most terrifying feeling in the world.

Gray fucked him faster and faster until Mason was shoving back against Gray then forcing his cock into Jack's hand. Jack managed to get a grip on both their cocks and worked them as fiercely as he could with his hand trapped between their bodies.

"Gonna come, Gray. Gonna any second," Jack hollered.

"You wanna fuck him?" Gray whispered in Mason's ear.

He made a choked sound. "Oh God, yes"

Gray pulled out of Mason. He handed Mason a condom, but Mason was too clumsy with need to open it. He rose up on his knees and let Jack sheath him while Gray lubed Jack's ass. Then Mason was sinking into Jack's heat. His tight ass felt like heaven.

Gray pushed back into Mason, and with each stroke, he drove Mason into Jack. Mason was caught between them, linked with them, and it was exactly what he wanted.

He must have hit Jack's sweet spot because Jack's eyes rolled back in his head, and he wrapped his hand around his cock. He pumped himself, fast. Mason pushed his hand away and took over.

One more deep thrust and Jack was coming. As his ass squeezed Mason's cock Mason tensed and fire lit up his whole body. His balls tightened impossibly, and he screamed, bucking against Jack as he filled the condom. Gray held onto his hips, grinding into him, hollering incomprehensible words as he came too. They all collapsed then, and Gray rolled to the side, pulling Mason with him.

"Bed now," Gray said as he disposed of his own condom then helped Mason with his.

Mason came up on his knees as Gray tossed the rubbers in the trash. He swayed, pitched forward, and caught himself on his hands. Gray lifted him and started toward the door.

"Be there in a minute," Jack mumbled.

Mason whimpered when Gray deposited him in bed and started to walk away.

"I'll be back," Gray assured him. "I just have to get Jack. I'm afraid he fell asleep. Otherwise, I'd never leave you like this."

Mason lay there, trying to figure out what was wrong with him. If Gray and Jack sent him home, he'd start crying again, like he had after Gray had spanked him. He needed to be wrapped up in them, but this was just sex. It was supposed to be just sex.

Gray guided Jack through the doorway and pushed him onto the bed. He mumbled something as he slid under the covers and pulled Mason to him.

Gray got in bed on the other side and spooned his big body around Mason. Mason cuddled back into him. He was warm and furry like a big bear. He wrapped himself around Jack and pillowed his head on Jack's shoulder.

"Shouldn't stay," he mumbled, but nothing short of force would make him leave.

"Hush," Gray said.

"Ridiculous." Jack's voice was clouded with sleep. "Belong here."

If only he did.

*****

Mason awoke to the sensation of someone running a hand up and down his chest, brushing lightly over his nipples, teasing his abdomen, circling his navel. He tried to open his eyes, but bright sun streamed in the window. Sun? It was morning?

He looked at the clock, blinking to make his eyes focus. "What time is it?"

"About 7:30," Jack responded, continuing to caresses him, dipping lower, making his cock stir.

Gray was sound asleep on his back on the other side of Mason. One of Mason's hands lay against his furry chest.

"AM?"

"Yes," Jack laughed.

"We never ate the tiramisu." Mason said the first thing that came to his mind.

"No, we didn't," Jack agreed, reaching between his legs and stroking his cock. "We could have it for breakfast, or…I could just have you."

Mason drew in a breath. He wanted that, wanted Jack's mouth around him, wanted to have them both again. He was addicted to them.

Jack tugged on his balls, making him groan. "Lie on your back."

Mason did as Jack asked. Then Jack positioned himself between Mason's legs. He went to work on Mason's cock with his to-die-for mouth, swallowing Mason all the way down. The slick heat of his throat made Mason whimper. He wasn't going to last long.

Gray stirred then. He rolled to his side and shoved the covers off them so he could watch Jack. Mason looked down too. The sight of Jack's mouth stretched over his cock had him thrusting up into him, begging for more.

Gray wrapped his right hand around his own cock and stroked himself. "What a sight to wake up to," he murmured.

Mason watched him until Jack increased his suction and Mason's eyes closed. All he could do was feel.

Jack teased Mason's balls with one hand and reached between his legs with the other. When he worked a finger past the tight muscles of his anus, Mason's body lit up. Jack pushed deeper into him, never stopping the crazy things he was doing with his mouth. He'd never…dear God…Jack curled his finger against Mason's prostate and that was all it took. His balls drew up tight, and he shot into Jack's willing mouth.

Gray groaned. "So fucking good. You two are doing me in."

When Jack had licked Mason clean, he rose up on his knees and turned to Gray. Gray got on his knees too and grabbed Jack's cock, which jutted out from his body, red and needy. Gray rubbed their cocks together as he possessed Jack with a ferocious kiss.

Mason reached between them, capturing their cocks in his hand and stroking them.

"Yes," Gray groaned. He tipped his head back, and Jack nibbled on his throat while both men thrust into Mason's tight grip.

Mason bent, pushing between them, making them readjust their position so he could lick the tips of their cocks as he jacked them off. He pushed his tongue into Jack's slit then into Gray's, eliciting groans and curses from both men. He ran the flat of his tongue over both of them, stroking them faster and faster, eager to taste their mingled cum.

He didn't have to wait long.

Gray laid one of his strong hands on Mason's head. His fingers dug in as he cried out and started to come. Jack joined him seconds later, squeezing Mason's shoulder like he needed to brace himself so he wouldn't fall.

Mason took the tips of both their cocks in his mouth and drank down all he could from each of them. It was messy and crazy and some of the most fun he'd ever had. When they'd recovered enough, they looked at the mess they'd made of each other and laughed.

"Shower," Gray grunted and stood, obviously expecting them to follow.

Jack smoothed Mason's hair and cupped his face. "You okay?"

Mason nodded. For the moment he was. He couldn't fight his attraction anymore. While expecting them to fall in love with him was ridiculous, and entertaining the idea of a three-way becoming a relationship was even more so, it was clear that he was more to them than a quick fuck. They wanted friendship, and they cared for him. That had to be enough for now. He was going to let things run their course, even if he ended up devastated in the end.

Chapter Eleven

Over the next month as spring brought the city to life, Mason continued to awaken under Gray's and Jack's touches and to find parts of himself he'd tried to shut down. He didn't like needing anyone the way he'd come to need them. He'd managed on his own just fine since he'd decided to make his own choices rather than letting his family direct his life. Of course that meant he was often lonely, but if he didn't expect anything from anyone else, he wouldn't be disappointed. Unconditional love wasn't something he believed in anymore, and yet Gray and Jack gave without his ever asking. They gave friendship and comfort in the form of food and cuddles on the couch and someone to listen when he had a bad day, and they gave blinding, mind-blowing pleasure without ever making demands on him.

Sex with them was always incredible, but it wasn't always kinky. Gray admitted that being a dominating bastard came naturally to him, but only when they all agreed did he expect obedience from them in the bedroom. Sometimes they had joke-filled, companionable sex or soothing, comforting sex after a difficult day, but the sex where Gray gave Mason both pain and pleasure was so intense it threatened to tear him asunder. They opened him up and saw right down to his core. That wasn't something he could handle every day.

And they didn't just fuck, they hung out together and talked. Mason even convinced Jack and Gray to spend a Saturday having a *Stargate* marathon, and by the end they were as caught up in the exploits of SG-1 as he was.

The robberies in the neighborhood around Nathan's stopped for several weeks, but the police believed the same group was responsible for incidents in another part of town even though the pattern wasn't exactly the same. The lack of well-organized robberies didn't slow down work for Jack and Gray though. They still worked the occasional double shift, and Mason often ended up seeing them only in the middle of the night.

Even still, he spent several nights each week at their house and he finally quit thinking he should leave every night. He kept a toothbrush there and a few changes of clothes. They talked about the three of them like they were a unit, but he kept waiting for things to end, for Jack and Gray to miss it being just the two of them. Because this couldn't possibly last. His lovers were a couple, and he was the guy they were fucking to spice things up.

That's how it had to be, didn't it? The three of them actually having a relationship was far too complicated. A few times Mason almost questioned his lovers about what they wanted from him, where they saw things going, but he always chickened out. He was certain if he started a conversation like that things would get weird, and everything would fall apart. He was terrified of what that would do to him. He'd tried to fight his dependence on them, but he couldn't stop himself from wanting them. Whenever they called, he came running, but he never initiated their nights together, until one night when he was so desperate for a friend that he had to call them.

His phone buzzed while he was working. He ignored it, because he had a line of customers at the bar. When the crowd finally died down, he pulled his phone out to check the missed calls and saw his mom's number. She was probably calling with yet another reminder about the anniversary party she was throwing for his sister. For some reason, despite the fact that no one in his family accepted him, they still expected him to attend this fanfare for his sister and her conservative lobbyist husband.

Despite her political affiliations, his mother's primary objection to Mason's being gay was more about the social inconvenience it presented her rather than any moral objection. As long as he didn't actually mention being gay or act gay or look gay, she could care less where his dick had been. When he was nineteen, he decided that his family's "Don't Ask Don't Tell" policy wasn't working for him, and he stopped attending his mother's soirees. Then a year and a half ago, his sister got engaged, and suddenly he was expected to be a dutiful son again even though they'd cut him off financially. He often regretted that he lived so close to them. Their house in Raleigh was only a half hour's drive from his apartment.

He knew whatever his mother had to say would piss him off, but he also knew she'd keep calling if he didn't deal with her so when he had a break, he steeled himself and listened to her voice mail. As usual, the message was vague, asking him to call her back and not explaining what she wanted.

He sighed and tapped her number on the screen.

She answered right away like she was sitting by the phone. Most likely she was at the kitchen bar with her five o'clock gin and tonic, going through a list of preparations for his sister's party.

"What did you need, Mom?"

She huffed. "Really, Mason. I taught you better manners than that. You could at least say hello."

"Hello, Mom. What did you need? I'm at work."

"I'm sure they can spare you for a few minutes."

He took a slow breath and willed myself not to get angry. "I'm on my break. When it ends they will in fact need me. The after-work crowd is coming in now."

"I've found you a date for Lisa's party."

My heart started to pound. She really hadn't gone there, had she? "Who is he?"

"*She* is the daughter of the new partner at your father's firm, the one I'd hoped to introduce you to at New Year's but you had to work at the last minute."

Mason had volunteered to work New Year's Day to avoid the dinner with his parents once he'd figured out it was another attempt to set him up with a woman.

"I do not require a date for this party."

"Can't you act reasonably, just this once?" Her voice was clipped and sharp.

"If by reasonably you mean not yelling at anyone when they refuse to listen to me when I've told them repeatedly that I'm gay and I do not date women, then yes. If you mean pretending to be straight to please you, then no."

"Can't you let your sister enjoy her celebration?"

"I don't see how my showing up without a date will ruin the celebration. It's not like I'm going to bring a stripper and have him blow me at the dinner table."

"Mason!" His mother pretended to be shocked.

"I won't change who I am to placate you or Lisa or your conservative friends."

"How long are you going to keep this up?"

Anger threatened to boil over. "Keep what up?" Mason's words were as sharp as his mother's had been.

"This gay thing."

Mason's fingernails bit into his palm. His other hand squeezed the phone so hard, he was lucky it didn't break. "This is who I am and who I'll be for the rest of my life."

His mother sighed. "Why do you need to make everything complicated?"

Mason was so mad his hands shook. "I will not be attending Lisa's party."

Before his mother could respond, he ended the call. Only the expense of replacing it kept him from throwing his phone across the room. He punched the wall instead.

Fitting In

As he flexed his hand, shaking off the ache from connecting with solid plaster, he realized he had to call Jack and Gray. They were off that night, and he'd planned to go over after work but he needed to talk to them now.

With shaky fingers, he pulled his phone back out and found Jack's number in his contacts. He was more likely to have his phone with him than Gray was. Just as he started to dial, Gwen stuck her head in the break room. "We're waiting for you out here."

He glanced at his watch. He still had a few minutes. Why the fuck did she have to be so pushy. "I'll be there in a minute," he growled.

She rolled her eyes and walked out. Jack answered then and he forgot all about bitchy waitresses.

"Are you guys home?" he blurted out without saying hello. Maybe his mom was right, he didn't have any manners.

"What's wrong?" Jack asked.

Even though he'd called because he needed to talk to someone, he was tempted to say nothing. "I'm okay. It's just that my mom called and—"

His voice broke. He wasn't sure why her attitude was hitting him so hard this time. She'd never understood him. Why would she start now?

"Mason?"

"I-I'm here. I just…"

"What did she say to you?" Jack's voice was low and overly calm. Mason could tell that he was ready to leap to Mason's defense, and it made him feel much better.

"The usual—why can't I just get over being gay, why can't I—" An embarrassing sob slipped out, and tears stung the back of Mason's eyes. He was not going to fucking cry. Not here at work. What the hell was wrong with him? He'd known his mother was selfish. He'd known she didn't care about his feelings, about who he really was. Why did it still hurt so much?

"We're coming to get you."

Mason sniffed and wiped at his eyes with his free hand. "I'm working."

"Tell them you don't feel good, and you have to leave early."

Mason ran a hand through his hair. He couldn't just leave work because his mom was an insensitive bitch. "I don't think—"

"You should not be making drinks right now."

He sighed. His hands were still shaking, and Mason knew he wouldn't be able to focus on work. "You're right."

"Of course I am," Jack said, the humor back in his voice. "And I bet you haven't taken a sick day in months."

Actually, he'd never taken one. "I'll try to get someone to fill in then come over."

"You will be leaving as soon as we get there." It was Gray. He must have grabbed the phone from Jack.

"What will everyone think if you march in here and extract me?" Mason wouldn't put it past Gray to just throw him over his shoulder and haul him out of the bar if he were worked up enough.

"That I came to pick up a friend who's not feeling good. And if they think something else, fuck it! You're more important."

His words made Mason's heart skip a beat. "God, Gray, I—"

"Tell your boss you're leaving."

There was no point in arguing with Gray. Ever. "Okay."

*****

Mason was sitting at one of the back tables tearing a napkin apart when Gray walked in, scanned the room, and stalked his way.

"Let's go," he said, his voice gruff. Tension rolled off him, and he didn't look Mason in the eye.

He looked like he needed comforting as badly as Mason did. If he didn't know Gray better, he'd think the man was pissed at him, but he'd learned that Gray acted like this when he was hurting. Mason longed to reach for him, to be folded in his arms, but they couldn't do that here. They weren't free to touch in public. When they stepped outside, he saw Gray's SUV in the parking lot. His bike was attached to the rack on the back. Apparently Gray didn't actually need a key to get the lock off. He expected to see Jack sitting in the passenger seat, but he wasn't there.

Before he could ask, Gray said, "I told Jack to stay at home and have some dinner ready for you."

Mason loved how Gray knew what he needed and how Jack used food to comfort people. "Thanks." Mason realized he'd never been alone with Gray before. He took a deep breath, drawing in his rich, musky scent. He was unexplainably nervous without Jack's easy chatter to break the tension.

When Gray had pulled away from the curb, he grabbed Mason's hand. "I'm sorry."

"For what?"

"For whatever has you looking so haunted and for not being able to comfort you in there."

"But I…I never expected you to."

Gray blew out a harsh breath. "I don't know how much longer I can stand the hiding."

Mason squeezed Gray's hand tightly. "I'm so sorry you have to."

Gray shook his head. "You're the one who's hurting and here you are trying to comfort me. I suck at this."

Mason shook his head. "No, you don't. I've never felt more taken care of than when I'm with you."

"I try." Gray didn't say anything else the rest of the drive.

When they went in, Jack had chicken and dumplings and green beans ready for them. Mason made his way to the table in a daze from the call with his mom and the intensity of emotion Gray had shown.

Gray sat down across from him, and Jack brought his own plate and joined them. "Let's eat and then you can tell us what happened."

Mason nodded.

Jack kept enough conversation going to keep an awkward silence from settling over them, but he didn't talk about anything significant other than telling Mason that another robbery had occurred near Nathan's. The police were worried that the criminals were moving their operation back to Jack and Gray's precinct.

When they finished eating and were all having a second beer, Mason told them what his mother had said and how he'd ended the call. He didn't cry again. In fact, he managed to repeat her words with very little emotion.

Jack laid his hand on Mason's arm. "I'm so sorry."

"You did the right thing. You shouldn't change for anyone." Gray's voice was strained. Mason looked up at him and noticed that his eyes were shiny with unshed tears.

"Oh, Gray."

Gray squeezed his eyes shut for a few seconds, obviously trying to get control of himself. Then he looked at Jack. "He's proud of who he is and he's not afraid to be honest about himself even when it might mean losing his family. When I went to get him, I couldn't touch him, couldn't hold his hand, couldn't hug him, couldn't scoop him up in my arms and take care of him the way I wanted to."

Mason reached across the table and grabbed Gray's hand. "It's fine, really. I didn't expect you to do those things. It's not like we're even really—"

Gray glared at Mason and jerked his hand back. Mason knew immediately that he'd said the wrong thing.

"It's not like we're even what?" Gray demanded.

Mason's voice shook as he spoke. "Dating."

Gray pushed back his chair and stood. Then he grabbed his beer bottle and threw it. It hit the kitchen wall and crashed to the floor. "What the fuck are we doing then? Fucking? Is that all you think this is?"

Gray had been pissy with Mason plenty of times but he'd never seen his lover this angry. If he hadn't known for sure that Gray wouldn't hurt him, he'd have been terrified.

Jack stood up and moved in front of Gray. "Go take off your clothes and lay on the bed." His voice held every bit as much command as Gray's did when he took control. Mason stared, unable to believe what Jack had said. Had he topped Gray before?

Gray's eyes widened as he looked down at Jack.

Mason stood, afraid of how Gray might react to Jack's demand. Should he offer to leave? Would that make things better or worse?

"Gray, you know you need this," Jack said, his voice softer now.

"Fuck!" Gray spat out the word.

Jack didn't back down. "Go to the bedroom. Now."

Gray turned and stomped down the hall.

Mason wanted to run and Jack must have sensed it, because he grabbed Mason's arm and held on tight.

"Sometimes all the responsibility he takes on gets to be too much for him. I know you're hurting, and you're confused but…."

Mason realized he couldn't leave, not when Gray was freaking out, not when he needed both of them so desperately. "I'll stay. I shouldn't be alone right now anyway."

Jack smiled softly. "No, you shouldn't. If I had my way, you wouldn't ever be alone."

What exactly does he mean by that? Does he want to try to make this be a real relationship? Does Gray? Do I?

Mason followed Jack to the bedroom and tried not to think too hard about those questions.

Chapter Twelve

Gray lay on the bed spread-eagle, naked, and hard, his hand sliding slowly up and down his shaft. His expression showed that he was pissed off, but his body didn't seem to care.

Jack climbed onto the bed next to him and stroked his thigh. "Relax and let us take care of you. We'll work everything out, but for now, just let go."

Gray shook his head. "Not that easy."

"No, it's not easy, but you can do it. Tell us what you need."

"You." He looked at Mason then, his eyes dark with emotion. "Both of you."

Mason started to undress. He needed them too, needed the slide of skin on skin. He needed to forget his fucked-up family, to forget that he was scared to death of how deep his feelings for Jack and Gray went, of how he'd come to depend on them being there, of how what they were doing went way beyond sex no matter what he tried to tell Gray.

Jack rubbed his cock through his jeans as he watched Mason strip. Mason wished suddenly that Jack and Gray were in uniform. He seriously needed something to distract him, and the idea of playing the badass criminal who'd taken a cop hostage turned him on like crazy.

Jack grinned. "Whatever you're imagining, file it away for another day. Right now I want you on this bed sucking Gray."

Mason swallowed. He loved the feel of Gray's thick cock in his mouth and the challenge it presented. Every time he sucked Gray off, he managed to take a little more of him down his throat.

Gray moaned and pushed harder into his own hand.

"Hands here." Jack tapped the headboard, and Gray growled.

"Do it."

Gray glared at Jack, but he reached up and wrapped his hands around two of the wooden slats in the headboard. As Mason settled beside Gray on the bed, he wondered how long it would take Gray to snap them in two.

Mason turned his attention to Gray's thick cock. He licked his way up to the head in long, slow strokes, like a cat cleaning itself. Gray bucked up, trying to get more contact.

Jack slapped the side of Gray's ass. "Keep still. Let him play with you."

"Fuck you!"

"That's fuck you, sir." Jack laughed as he took one of Gray's nipples between his thumb and forefinger. He tugged and pinched mercilessly on the already-puckered flesh.

Mason lifted Gray's shaft with his right hand and teased Gray's other nipple with his left. Gray rumbled, like a bear warning them that he was about to chase them down and rip them apart.

"You need this," Jack insisted.

Mason flicked his tongue across the tip of Gray's cock, tasting his pre-cum before pushing into the slit. Gray gasped.

Loving Gray's reaction, Mason took him into his mouth a little and sucked gently.

"Don't fucking tease me," Gray protested.

Jack shifted to straddle him, and Mason kept up his light sucking. He let go of Gray's nipple after giving it a hard tug that forced a hiss from the big man and shifted position so he could cup Gray's balls. Then he rolled them gently, letting his fingers slip back farther, seeking Gray's hole.

"I think your mouth needs something to do besides complain," Jack said.

Mason watched as Jack rose up and brushed the tip of his cock over Gray's lips. Gray opened, and Jack pushed in. Gray took him in, groaning as he started to suck. Jack lowered himself, forcing Gray to swallow him deeper.

Mason gripped his own cock. He wasn't going to last long watching them. Gray made a strangled sound around Jack as Mason focused again on giving Gray pleasure. Mason took him as deep as he could and stroked the rest of his shaft with one hand while using the other to alternately tease Gray's entrance and balls. Gray's thrusts became wilder as did the slurping and sucking sounds he was making as Jack fucked his mouth.

Gray's utter abandonment to pleasure was hot as hell. Mason desperately needed to come, but he wanted Gray to lose it first. He wanted to give him as much pleasure as Gray had given Mason over the last few months.

"You're about to come, aren't you?" Jack asked.

Gray must have given an affirmative answer because Jack's next words were. "Mason, stop."

Mason didn't want to let go of Gray's cock. He wanted to see if he could swallow every drop when Gray shot down his throat. But Jack probably had a plan for something even hotter. With a last, deep suck that had Gray gasping, he pulled off, and Gray's cock came free of his mouth with a loud pop.

Mason looked up to see Jack smiling at him over his shoulder. "He feels so good in your mouth, doesn't he?"

Mason nodded.

"But I don't want him to come in your mouth. I want him impaled on your cock when he shoots. He needs to know you care enough about him to give him exactly what he needs."

Mason stared at Jack, wide-eyed.

"Please," Gray's voice was filled with a desperation that made Mason shudder.

Dear God, Gray wants me to fuck him? He hadn't thought, hadn't realized Gray would want....

Jack tossed him lube and a condom, then he pulled his cock from Gray's mouth and shifted so Mason could watch Gray's face.

Gray reached for him, letting go of the headboard for the first time since Jack had told him not to move. Mason leaned down and let Gray cup his face. Gray kissed him, gently at first, but then

Gray opened and Mason swept his tongue into his mouth, tasting Jack there, and the kiss turned wild. They bit and licked and fought each other with their tongues.

Gray arched up, forcing their cocks together. The contact was enough to bring Mason dangerously close to the edge. How the hell was he supposed to last once he got inside Gray, inside the man who had captivated him in ways he didn't have words for? Gray might be stoic most of the time, but that night his emotions were right at the surface, and Mason longed to soothe all his hurt. Somehow he knew that doing so would make his own wounds start to heal.

"Shouldn't have said anything. Not when you're the one who's been hurt," Gray said against his lips.

"I would rather help you than talk about my stupid family."

"Fuck me, please."

Gray begging was almost more than Mason could handle. "God yes."

Suddenly Mason want to fuck Gray more than he would have thought possible. He loved it when Gray told him what to do, when he gave him just enough pain to help him sink into a place free of worry and tension, then fucked him so hard he couldn't breathe. But the thought of feeling Gray's ass clamped around his dick had him shaking with need.

He slicked up a few fingers and pushed one into Gray before quickly adding another, pushing deeper, loving the look of ecstasy on Gray's face.

"Need you. Now." Gray's words came out growly, demanding.

Jack leaned down and kissed Gray as Mason pulled on a condom, lubed his cock, and positioned himself at Gray's entrance.

Gray pushed at Jack. "Need to see him when he fucks my ass."

Jack sat back, grinning. Mason pulled Gray's legs around him and drove forward.

"Fuck!" Gray cried.

His tight ass gripped Mason's cock so hard it hurt. "You ok?" Mason asked.

Sweat dripped down Gray's face, but he nodded. "Never better."

Mason looked over at Jack, afraid he might be upset by Gray's words, but Jack was smiling.

"I want you inside me," Mason said to Jack.

"Later. You both need this right now."

Mason nodded, incapablc of saying more. He pulled back, struggling against Gray's effort to hold him inside. Then he thrust until he was balls-deep in Gray's ass. The look of wonder on Gray's face was so beautiful. Part of Mason wanted to stay suspended like that forever, but his cock needed friction, and it needed it right then. He started fucking Gray as slowly as he could. But soon he couldn't help himself. He started driving against Gray, hard and fast. "Can't. Hold. Back."

Gray growled. "Harder."

Mason groaned and let go completely.

Gray wrapped a hand around his own cock and worked himself as Mason fucked him. They kept up a wild rhythm until Gray's ass fluttered around Mason's cock, and his legs tensed.

Mason drove in as hard as he could, and Gray cried out as he climaxed, shooting across his chest and up to his chin. Jack leaned down and started cleaning him with his tongue.

The sight of Jack's tongue licking up Gray's cum did Mason in. Mason gave one final thrust and screamed Gray's name as he slammed his hips against his lover and came.

He fell forward over Gray, no longer able to support himself. Jack sat back, and Gray held Mason, wrapping his strong arms around him and sighing.

*****

Mason heard the sound of a condom wrapper tearing then the snick of the lube being opened and the sluicing of lubed fingers sliding along skin.

The bed dipped, and he turned just enough to see Jack behind him.

"You still want this?" Jack asked, hand stroking his cock.

Mason's cock twitched at the sight of Jack there, dick in hand, ready to fuck him. He wasn't sure he could survive any more pleasure, but hell yeah, he wanted it.

"Yes." The word was breathy, barely there. Jack smiled. "Good."

Mason expected Jack to push right into him with no prep. Instead, Jack pulled Mason up onto his knees, spread his cheeks, and licked him from his balls to the top of his ass. When Jack pushed his tongue against Mason's pucker, he gasped and pushed back against him, his dick starting to swell again though he would have thought that impossible.

Gray tightened his hold on Mason. "His tongue feels incredible, doesn't it? I love when he eats my ass. He pushes in so deep, slicks me up, and then fucks me hard and rough. He's amazing when he goes all dominant."

Mason raised up enough to look at Gray. Questions swirled through his mind. "I thought...."

"Variety is good," Gray said, grinning.

"Ye—" He choked as Jack pushed into him with his warm tongue. "Incredible."

Jack teased him, tongue-fucked him, licked all around his hole, and then finally his cock was there, driving in. Gray was right. He wasn't gentle, but Mason didn't care. He didn't want gentle. He wanted Jack to use him. To make him feel it. To make him remember it for days.

Jack dug his fingers into Mason's hips as he thrust deep, filling him completely in a single stroke.

Mason cried Jack's name. He was instantly rock hard and ready to come again.

Jack didn't give him time to adjust. He pulled back and thrust again, and he kept up a ferocious rhythm that made Mason fight for each shallow breath. He wasn't going to last long. The heat, the need, the.... His balls tightened. Lightning sizzled down his back, setting him on fire. He shouted incomprehensible things as Gray held him tight, and he came just as Jack bucked against his ass and found his own peak.

Jack landed on top of him, pushing him farther into Gray, and wrapped his arms around both of them. "You're amazing."

"Mmm. I lov—"

Oh God, what had he done? His head swam; his gut clenched in horror. He caught himself before he finished the statement, but they had to know what he'd almost said.

He struggled to free himself, but Gray held him tight and stroked his head. "It's okay."

What did that mean? If he realized what Mason almost said, how could it be okay? How could things ever be okay?

Jack laid his head on Mason's back and kissed him over and over like he was trying to soothe him.

But Mason needed to get away. He needed to be somewhere they couldn't touch him so he could think. He tried again to extract himself from between them. Finally, he got out the words "bathroom, please" in a choked voice.

Gray slowly slid his hands down Mason's back, squeezed his ass and then let go. Jack sat back, but when Mason rose, he grabbed him and kissed him before he could run. What if it was their last kiss?

Mason heard Jack and Gray murmuring to each other as he closed the door to the en suite. He couldn't let himself think about what they were saying.

Mason stood at the sink, avoiding looking at himself in the mirror. He didn't want to see the fear in his eyes.

He turned on the cold water and splashed some on his face, trying to cool the burn of humiliation. Jack and Gray tore away all his defenses and made him feel things too strongly. He'd known they'd be trouble from the moment he started crushing on them. But he hadn't thought it would be this bad. And now he'd fucked everything up. Or had he? Why hadn't they seemed shocked or upset?

Why had Gray gotten angry when Mason suggested they weren't really dating? What did he think they were doing?

Ask. This wasn't the first time his subconscious had suggested talking to them about where their relationship was going.

He responded as he always had. *Fuck no. Then run away. You're good at that.*

"Fucking bastard." Mason bit his lip when he realized he'd said the words out loud. He hoped Gray and Jack hadn't heard him.

He took a deep breath, risked a glance in the mirror, and noticed bite marks on his neck. He barely remembered Gray biting him as Jack made him lose his mind with his punishing thrusts. Fear had made the color drain from his face. He'd look like a vampire's victim if Gray's teeth were a bit pointier.

He shook his head at the thought. He was losing his mind. He needed to get out of there before he did something else stupid.

He wet a washcloth with warm water, cleaned himself up, then got washcloths for Gray and Jack. He reached for the doorknob, vowing to act normal, to tell them calmly that he should go. He wasn't really running away. He was just giving himself some healthy distance.

Sure you are.

Fuck off.

He stepped out of the bathroom. Gray and Jack were cuddled on the bed, Jack's head on Gray's chest. They looked so peaceful, so right. He wasn't going to let himself come between them.

He handed them both a washcloth then picked up his pants. "I should go. I…I've got a lot to think about." That wasn't a lie. He didn't want to lie to them, but the whole truth…he couldn't tell that either.

Gray looked hurt. "Stay." His harsh, one-word command let Mason know he was upset.

Jack sat up but kept a hand on Gray's chest as he watched Mason. "Remember what you said earlier. You shouldn't be alone tonight."

"I needed this, you, to be touched, cared for. But now I need to think. I'm…I just need to think."

Jack looked scared. Mason had never seen him so lacking in confidence, and it made him afraid too. Gray looked ready to grab Mason, drag him down to the bed, and hold him there until he relented.

"Look, I'll call, I just…." Why the fuck did it sound like he was saying goodbye?

Jack shook his head, the look of horror still there. Did he know Mason might not come back, that this might be it?

"Don't" was all he said.

"I have to."

Gray turned away and buried his face in a pillow.

Jack narrowed his eyes at Mason, angry now. "Be sure you know what you're doing."

"I...please...I just can't."

Jack sighed, and it was all Mason could do to keep from climbing on the bed and pulling both of them into his arms.

"Be careful," Jack said. "Did you bike to work?"

"Yeah." Gray had fixed his car a few weeks after they'd started sleeping together, but it still acted up occasionally, and he liked saving gas money by biking anyway.

"Take my car," Gray said, his voice muffled by the pillow.

Mason shook his head. "No, I can't do that."

"God damn it! Just take it." Gray still didn't look at Mason, but the pain and anger in his voice frightened him.

"His keys are in the bowl by the door," Jack said. "One of us will pick them up from you at Nathan's tomorrow."

Jack gave him a pleading look, and Mason couldn't argue with him anymore. "Fine."

Mason pulled on his t-shirt and grabbed his button-down. Then he pushed his feet into his shoes, not bothering to put them on properly, just mashing the backs down with his heels. He had to get out of there. Seeing these two strong men look so sad, so defeated, was killing him, but what could he do? How could he stop this?

"Text me when you get home so we know you're safe, okay?"

Mason nodded, unable to speak. His chest was so tight he could barely breathe. If he could just make it to Gray's car…

He grabbed his bag and Gray's car key and raced out the door, slamming it closed behind him as his tears spilled over and slid down his face. At least it was dark so no one could see him clearly. He managed to get the SUV unlocked so he could fold himself into the driver's seat. The seats smelled like Gray, a scent he'd come to think of as comforting. Now it just reminded him of all he'd lost. He laid his head over the steering wheel and sobbed. When he was wrung out and hollow inside, he started the car, backed out of the driveway, and drove home.

When he pushed the door closed behind him, he crumbled to the floor. Hours later, he dragged himself to bed and fell into an exhausted sleep filled with dreams of his mom yelling at him, his dad giving him his characteristic concerned frown, his sister begging him to play along so they could all be happy, and Jack and Gray fucking each other in front of him, but just out of reach. Whenever he tried to get to them, he couldn't move forward, as if they were surrounded by a forcefield and he lacked the magic to break through.

Chapter Thirteen

Mason's heart rate accelerated when he saw Jack sitting in an out-of-the-way booth. Three days had passed since he'd fled their house. Three days with no contact other than the text he'd sent to let Jack know he'd gotten home safely. He'd made sure to arrange for them to pick up Gray's car key when he wasn't at Nathan's. Elizabeth, his manager, had taken care of the exchange without asking too many questions.

Then that morning he'd texted Jack and asked if they could meet him, because he wanted to talk. Jack had let him know that Gray had to go into work early to take care of some paperwork, but he'd offered to come by the bar before his shift started. And now he was here looking sexier than ever in his uniform and police hat.

Mason had realized he couldn't keep pretending he was going to magically become comfortable with the words he'd let slip. He hadn't meant to fall in love with Jack and Gray, and the best thing for all of them would be if he backed away before things got messy. Friends-with-benefits was one thing, but if Jack and Gray understood how he really felt about them, he risked fucking things up for all three of them. They deserved to go on, happy in their love for each other like they had been before he'd met them.

But now that Jack was there, Mason wasn't sure he could he make himself say what he needed to. Could he really look into Jack's sparkly blue eyes and say he didn't want to see Jack or Gray anymore? What choice did he have though? He'd saw the strain his leaving put on them after he'd almost confessed how he felt. So far he hadn't seen any signs that his being in their life had affected how Jack and Gray felt for each other, but the thought of them disagreeing over him, over how to respond to the fact that he was in love with them, terrified him. What if they stopped looking at each other with those soft, caring looks, with that need that went bone deep…. He wouldn't risk fucking up what they had by trying to push deeper into their lives.

As soon as he was able to take a break, Mason carried a beer over to Jack and slid into the booth opposite him.

Jack smiled. "Every time I see you, you get more beautiful."

Mason's cheeks heated. He glanced around, hoping for Jack's sake that no one had heard. Fortunately, it was a slow part of the day, and there were only a few other customers in the bar. None of them were nearby.

Jack took a sip of his beer and studied Mason with his cop face on. "What's wrong?"

Mason stared at the table. "I can't see you anymore." His voice was so low it was barely audible.

Pain flashed in Jack's eyes as he stared at Mason. "Why?" The word came out choked.

"I...I just can't."

Jack closed his eyes and rubbed at them with the heels of his hands. Mason's stomach flip-flopped.

"Did we push you too hard? Hurt you?" Jack asked.

Mason shook his head vigorously. "No, it's not you. It's me."

"What do you need? Just tell me and..." Jack looked down and played with the label on his bottle.

Mason took a deep breath, trying to steady himself. He'd known Jack would push. He was a cop after all. It was in his nature to interrogate. "I...things have been..." He paused after those false starts, trying to figure out what to say.

Jack didn't look at him.

Finally he said, "You and Gray, you've been wonderful, but when Gray asked what we were doing if we weren't dating, I didn't have a good answer, and I still don't. You two are so good together; I don't want to come between you."

"We both care for you."

Mason looked up. "You do?"

Jack tensed and his face hardened. He was pissed now. At least that was easier for Mason to deal with.

"Did you really think this was just about sex?"

"No. At first I did, but then, well, I realized you thought of me as a friend."

Jack shook his head as if Mason had said something supremely stupid. "Is that what you really think? Is that all this is to you? We're just fuck buddies?"

Jack froze, probably realizing how loud his voice had gotten. He glanced around, and Mason did too. There was still no one near them.

Mason turned toward the window and looked out at the quiet street. He was afraid if he looked at Jack, his resolve would crumble. The pain in Jack's eyes was too much.

"I'm sorry," Mason said. He slipped out of the booth and stood. "I can't risk ruining what you have with Gray or…."

"Or what?" Jack's words were harsh. "Risk admitting your own feelings?"

Tears stung the back of Mason's eyes. Jack was right. He wasn't willing to risk himself. Leaving was tearing him apart as it was. Letting himself feel more might just kill him.

"It was good while it lasted," he said.

Jack glared at him. Mason didn't think he'd ever seen him look that ferocious. He imagined it was how Jack would look if he were arresting someone for murder.

Mason started to walk away, but Jack grabbed his arm. "Is this really how you want to end it?"

Mason pulled free. "I've got customers waiting. I need to go." He didn't let himself look back as he headed to the bar. Later, when he glanced toward Jack's table, Jack was gone.

*****

Just over a week had gone by since Mason told Jack he couldn't see him and Gray anymore. They hadn't called, not that he'd expected them to. He certainly hadn't hoped they would. No, that was beyond foolish.

They hadn't been in the bar either, at least not when Mason was working, which was good. Not seeing them he could take; it was what he'd asked for, but having them come into Nathan's and not speak to him might do him in.

He'd been an ass to Jack, and he could only imagine how angry Gray had been when Jack had told him about the conversation. He was lucky Gray hadn't come after him for hurting Jack. He'd been cold, because he was trying to make walking away easier. If he'd let Jack see how much it cost him, he would probably have chickened out. He wondered if Jack had seen through the act, but it didn't matter; he'd ended things with them and that was for the best, even if right then he felt like only half a person.

The first few days after he'd broken things off, he'd picked up his phone at least once an hour, ready to call Jack and apologize, but each time he stopped himself because if he did, he would end up begging to see them again. He worried that if Gray and Jack came in for a drink he'd rush over to them and confess exactly how he felt about them. Because every second of every day he craved them, body and soul.

And just when he'd thought he might be doing a little better because he'd gotten through the busiest part of the night without scanning the tables a single time looking for Jack and Gray, he got home and found a letter waiting for him that hit him like a punch to the gut. Test results. He knew Gray and Jack didn't use condoms when it was just the two of them, and when things seemed to be going so well, he'd decided to get tested and then see how they felt about going bare with him.

His hands shook as he opened the envelope, not because he was worried he wasn't clean, but because now he'd never know what it felt like to have their naked cocks inside him. He'd never shared that level of trust with anyone.

He unfolded the letter. He was clean. If only…. No, he couldn't think about it. Wet spots began to appear on the paper. Mason wiped at his tears, but they fell faster and faster. Who the fuck cried because they got a clean bill of health? He sank to his knees on his kitchen floor and wondered if he'd ever recover from this fuckup.

He moved through the next day like a zombie. He fucked up more drinks orders in a few hours than he had in the previous year. Elizabeth, his manager, had bitched at him, and when Mason meekly apologized, she asked if something was wrong. He told her he was having some family problems, which was true enough. Jack and Gray weren't the only people he hadn't talked to in the last two weeks. Unlike them though, his mother had called no less than five times, leaving messages about the party, as if their conversation about his "gay phase" had never happened.

Elizabeth tried to send him home to get some rest, but Mason had pleaded with her to let him stay. The last thing he'd wanted was to be home alone where he thought of nothing but Jack and Gray. The only thing that had kept him from driving over to their house the night before to see if they would take him back was his fear that they had found someone to take his place. His stomach plummeted at the thought and the pint glass he was holding slid from his fingers and shattered against the side of the sink.

Mason stared at the broken glass, fighting the despair that threatened to overtake him and hoping he wasn't going to have to rush to the bathroom to vomit. His family couldn't accept him for who he really was. He had acquaintances at work, but he pushed away almost anyone who wanted to get close to him. He was used to being alone, but after Jack and Gray...alone had become lonely.

Jack and Gray had made him feel welcome. They'd cared about getting to know him. And he'd gotten used to having them to talk to. Even the nights he didn't spend with them, they often talked or texted, and though he'd tried not to until that awful night when his mom treated him like shit, he'd known he could call them if he needed something, anything, just like they were his...boyfriends?

Mason shook his head as he cleaned up the broken glass, cursing when he sliced his thumb open on one of the fragments. He'd just gotten the bleeding stopped when sirens blared and police cars went screaming by followed by an ambulance. The hairs on the back of his neck rose. He knew something truly awful had happened.

A man ran into the bar. "Some crazy ass just shot a cop right down the street," he yelled. Everyone started talking at once. Several people ran over to the window and just as many headed for the door, stepping out onto the sidewalk.

Mason stood at the bar, frozen. *Shot a cop. Shot a cop.* The words kept echoing in his head. Jack. Gray. He dropped the bloody rag he'd wrapped around his hand and took off running.

"Where the hell are you going?" Gwen asked as he pushed past her, nearly making her drop a tray.

He didn't respond. Once he was out on the sidewalk, he noticed that onlookers seemed to be coming from all over. A shooting sure did draw a crowd.

He saw crime scene tape up ahead. How far beyond was…the victim? His heart pounded. *Please, God, don't let it be Jack or Gray.*

"Excuse me." He cut between an elderly couple that were almost at the barrier. An officer stood on the other side of the tape, warning everyone to stay back.

"The officer who was shot," he demanded. "Who was it?"

"I'm not authorized to—"

"Please. I'm friends with…just please tell me."

Mason knew he sounded frantic, possibly psychotic.

"Step back, sir."

Mason forced himself to back away from the tape. He stood on tiptoe, trying to see, but there were paramedics and police swarming the area. He scanned the length of the tape barrier. Was there another spot where he might sneak through? Could he pretend to be someone official? An off-duty paramedic, maybe?

He sure as hell wasn't going to stand there and keep wondering or wait until he heard it on the news. He pushed back through the crowd until he got to the corner. Then he started down a side street. Maybe the barrier wouldn't be as hard to get through there.

He made his way through the crowd until he could see the crime scene tape. A paramedic leaned over a body on the ground. Mason watched him shake his head. Another man pulled a sheet up over the victim's face.

Oh God. He's dead. Whoever that is, is dead. Mason shook all over. His dinner threatened to come back up.

Then the whoop of another siren distracted him. A police car flew past him and came to a screeching halt. A big man jumped out leaving the door standing open. When he turned toward Mason, Mason realized it was Gray. Jack climbed out of the car a second later.

They were okay. They were really okay.

Mason's knees buckled and he stumbled, falling against a man who was standing by him. The man looked at him with disdain, probably thinking he was drunk.

He managed to right himself, but he was dizzy and shaky and half-sick. He wanted to get away, but he couldn't move. Gray looked right at him.

Mason lifted a hand and waved feebly. Gray didn't wave back. He put his arm around Jack's shoulder, and both men hurried through the crime tape. At least they could hug each other here. That would be expected in a time of grief.

Mason pulled out his phone and texted Jack. "I'm sorry I was an ass, and I'm sorry you lost someone today."

He doubted they'd respond, but he felt better for having done it. There wasn't anything else he could do right then, but at least he knew they were alive. They might have died without him seeing them again.

He'd made a mistake, a huge fucking mistake. He'd told himself he was saving them all from the greater pain of ending things down the road, but by backing off, he'd done nothing but hurt Jack, Gray, and himself. He remembered the look in Jack's eyes when he'd broken up with him. And it *was* a breakup whether Mason had wanted to admit it at the time or not. They had been in a relationship.

He'd been too afraid of what it would mean to try to make things work with three of them. There were people who had three-way relationships and made things work, but he didn't see how they did it. Dating was hard enough with just two, and while some of his reasons for ending things had been selfish, he honestly didn't want to come between the two of them. Their love for each other was so beautiful. Could they really have feelings for him like they did for each other, or would they always be a couple and he be their third?

If they were going to get jealous, don't you think you'd have seen it by now?

We were always together. What if I was with one of them?

What if you were?
Fuck!

He got back to Nathan's without remembering any of the journey. When he pushed the door open and stumbled in, Elizabeth was at the bar, but there were only a few customers. He guessed everyone had either gone to gawk at the crime scene or been deterred by the crowds, the police, or the potential danger.

Elizabeth glared at him. "What the fuck did you leave for?"

Gwen, the bitchy waitress who'd tried to stop him on his way out, rolled her eyes. "Seriously? Haven't you seen him cozying up to those two cops? He had to go check on his crushes."

Mason stepped right up to her, snarling. "Back off. A man was killed out there."

She stared back, then stepped away, hands up. "Fine. Just don't walk off and leave us again."

"Bitch," he spat at her retreating back.

"Yeah, she is, but you can't just run out," Elizabeth said.

"I thought...I had to know who it was."

Elizabeth nodded. "You're forgiven this time, but if it happens again, there will be serious consequences, got that?"

"Yeah. Thanks."

She patted him on the shoulder. "Go home, and if whatever has had you moping around here has to do those two gorgeous cops, fix it."

Mason started to argue, but Elizabeth shook her head. "I don't need to know about it. It's probably best if I don't. Just fix it."

"I'll try." He wished he knew how.

Chapter Fourteen

Once news about the shooting was released, Mason learned that the killer was suspected to be one of the members of the team who'd been robbing businesses close to Nathan's. Mason knew there had been another robbery just days before, and Elizabeth had reminded them all to be extra careful when they locked up at night, but so far he hadn't heard of anyone being hurt during the break-ins. If they'd thought his life was in danger, Jack and Gray would have warned him, wouldn't they?

Jack hadn't responded to Mason's text, not that Mason had really expected him to, but...well...he'd hoped. Mason supposed it was possible Jack still would contact him. The last three days couldn't have been easy for Jack and Gray. The funeral for the officer who was shot had taken place that morning, and Mason was sure the investigation was taking up most of their time while they still had to deal with other, more routine calls.

It was almost closing time on a Wednesday night. There were only a few hardcore drinkers left, so Mason got to work cleaning up and getting ready to shut things down. He wondered if Jack and Gray were working. The temptation to call and find out—assuming they'd take his call—was enormous.

Call.

Don't call.

Call.

Don't call.

He went back and forth about a hundred times. Finally he slipped away from the bar for a few seconds and placed his phone in his bag in the break room so the temptation was no longer in reach. He should give them more time and let them grieve for their friend. He wanted to fix things even if he just apologized for how he'd treated them at the end, but now wasn't the time to bother them.

Or maybe you're still too chicken.

No, that couldn't be it.

If they wanted to talk now, Jack would have texted back.

Mason tried to focus on cleaning up his area for the night. When the last customer finally left and Mason had locked the door behind him, he resisted the urge to run to his phone and call Jack and Gray. They were probably on duty anyway.

"They're onto me. I'm sure I was being followed. Let's just get out of here."

Mason froze. He'd thought he was alone, and he didn't recognize the voice.

"We're not leaving when we're this close. I've got a plan."

Gwen. Apparently she was still there, and she was talking to someone. He'd seen her leave work a few times with a skinny, ferret-faced man with thick, wavy brown hair that looked like it belonged on someone else's head. She must have had this boyfriend or whoever he was pick her up, but what did he mean about somebody being on to them?

Their conversation continued in lowered voices, and Mason went looking for them. Gwen needed to get out of there so he could close up and go home. When he opened the door to the kitchen, she turned toward him. "Don't move," she said.

Mason arched a brow. What the hell had gotten into her? "Why are you still here?" he asked.

She smiled, and Mason got the same feeling of unease he'd had when he heard sirens the night the cop had been shot.

Something wasn't right. He remembered telling Jack and Gray that Gwen had worked at Gino's until just before they were robbed. He started to back out of the room. Why the hell hadn't he kept his phone with him? Now would be the perfect time to call Jack or Gray.

The ferret-faced man pulled out a gun and aimed it at him. "She said don't move."

Mason stopped breathing. He stared at the gun. His family hadn't been handgun owners, and other than when he'd watched Jack and Gray clean their police-issue weapons and slip them into their holsters, he'd never been up close and personal with one. He'd certainly never had one pointed at him.

None of his self-defense moves were going to help him against a bullet. His stomach roiled, but he fought the nausea and his rising panic. He wasn't going to let Gwen and this asshole see how scared he was.

"What's going on?" he asked, being careful to stay completely still. He wanted answers, but he didn't want to spook this man who already seemed rather nervous judging by the way he kept bouncing on his toes and shifting his gaze from Gwen to Mason and back again.

"We're going to clear out the cash and the other valuables, and you're going to help us," Gwen said.

The bitchy waitress and her rodent-y boyfriend were the criminal masterminds behind the recent robberies? He'd told Jack and Gray he couldn't imagine Gwen being involved in the crimes, because he'd thought she was dumb as a stump, and now he might not live long enough to tell them he'd been wrong. More importantly, he might never be able to tell Jack and Gray that he loved them. Why hadn't he called them earlier? If he lived through this, there would be no more chickening out. He was going to tell them how he felt and beg them to give him a second chance.

The man looked at Gwen. "We need to get out of here now. I'm sure the cops are on to me."

Gwen snarled. "The cops don't know about me yet. We're going to clear this place out before we leave."

He shook his head. "You can't be sure what they know. We need to go."

Gwen proceeded to tell him exactly how stupid he was. While he was distracted, Mason considered charging him. The guy was rattled, and Mason had a decent chance of bringing him down without getting shot, but there was also a chance he'd be killed, so he hesitated, immediately wishing he hadn't. What were his chances of surviving the night anyway? He could identify Gwen and her boyfriend. One of them or their accomplices hadn't hesitated to kill a cop. They weren't going to get sentimental over a bartender.

Gwen gave up on arguing with Ferret Boy and focused on Mason. "You're going to open the safe for us."

He nodded in acquiescence, since there was no point in resisting. As long as he was needed, they'd keep him alive. Maybe he could get them distracted again and make a move. Or maybe, by some miracle, the police really were following the boyfriend, and they would trace him to Nathan's. There was a chance Jack and Gray had looked into Gwen since they'd made the connection of her moving from Gino's to Nathan's.

Mason pointed toward the office. "The safe's in there. Are you going to shoot me if I start walking?"

"No," Gwen answered even though she wasn't the one holding the gun. The man didn't seem inclined to do anything without her telling him to.

Mason walked slowly, hoping to hear a siren, longing for Jack and Gray to ride to the rescue. He was surprisingly calm as he pulled his keychain from his pocket and opened the cabinet that held the safe. He debated pretending to have forgotten the combination, but he doubted Gwen would buy it. Co-operation still seemed like the best strategy.

He turned the knob slowly, hoping Gwen's friend would get distracted, but he kept his gun trained on Mason, hardly even blinking.

"I guess you're really pleased with yourself, fooling Elizabeth and the rest of us," Mason said.

Gwen laughed. "It's amazing how gullible people are. This is the third bar or restaurant I've worked at in this neighborhood and still no hint that anyone suspects me."

Mason snorted. "I must say I'm shocked to find out you've got the brains to pull this off."

She crowded up behind him. "There are a few ways this night could end for you. Keep talking like that, and I'll pick the one that makes you suffer most."

"Just leave him alone so he can get the safe open." The man sounded agitated. Mason wondered if he could get him stirred up enough to make him bolt.

Mason made the last turn on the dial and heard the click that signaled the lock was open. He tugged and the door swung out, revealing the week's cash. Gwen had done her homework. Elizabeth always made a deposit on Monday. She'd waited until the best moment to make her play, but still the money was nothing compared to what they could get robbing a bank. "Why restaurants and small businesses? Don't you want to go for a bigger mark?"

Gwen just laughed. "What we want is to not get caught. These places have next to no security, as you can see, and we've easily taken a quite a pile."

"Easily? You killed a cop." Mason responded.

"The fool that did that has been taken care of."

Great. More evidence that they weren't afraid to kill.

"Take it out and put it in here." She handed Mason a duffle bag.

He did as she asked, working slowly, but not so slowly that she had a reason to complain. Ferret

Boy had lowered his gun, but he still had it in his hand, and he was watching Mason carefully. Mason wasn't sure if Gwen was armed or not. His odds were not good, but what were they if he did nothing?

Suddenly Gwen looked up from zipping the bag that now contained all the money from the safe. "What was that?"

Mason frowned. "What was what?"

"I heard something, like someone moving around outside." She looked up at Mason. "Is anyone else here?"

He shrugged. "I didn't even know you were here. As far as I knew I was alone."

She narrowed her eyes at him. "Were your cops coming to meet you after work?"

"They're not my cops, and no."

"I've seen how you look at them. There's something going on there."

Mason didn't respond.

"I'm going to check it out," she said. "Keep an eye on him."

Gwen stepped out of the windowless office, heading toward the kitchen. Mason wanted to get them out of the confined space. He needed more room for a fight. "There's more money in the till. I hadn't cleared it yet." He started out of the room, waiting for the man to try and stop him.

"Why are you being so helpful?" Ferret Boy asked.

"Gwen's going to ask for it eventually. We might as well get it while she's chasing noises."

He considered what Mason had said for a moment, then finally nodded. "Fine, let's get moving."

Mason did. When they reached the main room, he prepared himself to make a move. He needed to do something now, before Gwen came back.

He walked slowly toward the bar so the man would think he was going to empty the till like he'd said. When he glanced over his shoulder, the man gestured toward the bar, encouraging him to keep moving. His gun was in his hand, but it wasn't pointed at Mason.

This was it. Mason steeled himself to attack.

Then the door burst open. "Police. Drop your weapons and put your hands up."

Jack.

Ferret Boy brought his gun up, pointing it straight at Jack.

Mason whirled and kicked his arm. The gun went off as it flew from his hand, and a roar echoed in the room.

Before Mason could register what was happening, Gray was on top of Gwen's partner, pummeling him. He smashed his fist into the man's face again and again.

Mason tugged on his arm. "Gray! Gray!"

A detective Mason vaguely recognized as an occasional customer whistled loudly, and Gray froze. He blinked then looked Mason up and down. "Are you okay?"

"Yeah."

Ferret Boy stared up at Gray, looking terrified, blood running freely from his nose.

Gray looked back at Mason, and Mason knew he needed to get Gray up and out of there.

He tugged on his arm again, and Gray stood. Then Jack was there, reading Ferret Boy his rights.

"Gwen was working with him," Mason blurted out. "She went toward the back to investigate a noise."

"We got her," the detective said.

Mason looked at him, keeping a hand on Gray's arm.

"I'm Detective Marsh." He held his hand out to Mason.

It seemed a strangely civilized gesture after what had just happened. But after a few seconds of paralyzed uncertainty, Mason shook his hand. "Mason Shields."

"Are you all right?" Marsh asked.

Mason nodded. "Yeah, they just had me empty the safe, and Gwen took the money in a duffle."

"We have it."

Now that things were going to be okay, Mason started to shake, no longer able to hold himself together. Gray pulled off his jacket and wrapped it around Mason's shoulders. "Are you sure he didn't hurt you?"

"Yeah. He wanted to run, but Gwen wouldn't let him. She was the one in charge."

Mason glanced toward Ferret Boy. Jack had him cuffed and was in the process of pulling him to his feet. "Come on," Jack said to Gray. "We've got to get him to the station."

"Tell Anderson and Blaine to take the woman back, too," Detective Marsh said. "I'm going to get

Mr. Shields's statement and finish looking around here."

"I'm staying too," Gray said.

The detective shook his head. "No, you're not. After that display, you'll be lucky not to be facing suspension."

Gray looked at Mason. "Will you be okay if we leave?"

Mason nodded. He desperately wanted Gray and Jack to stay with him, but he knew they had to do things by the book. Gray had already stepped over the line by attacking Ferret Boy after he was disarmed, and he was dangerously close to outing himself with the tender looks he was giving Mason. Mason had no intention of making him lose his job.

"I'm fine. Go do what you need to do."

Gray studied him for a few seconds then nodded. "Okay, but…"

"I'll take good care of him," Detective Marsh said.

Gray looked at him. "You better."

Marsh shook his head as Gray and Jack walked out the door. Did he realize what was going on between the three of them? Mason wouldn't doubt he did. Jack and Gray's secret might not be a secret much longer.

Chapter Fifteen

Mason lay curled under a blanket on the couch, unable to stop shivering. Detective Marsh had dropped him off at home after taking his statement. He hadn't heard from Jack or Gray yet, and he wasn't sure when he would. They might be working until morning, especially if Gwen or Ferret Boy gave them the names of others they were working with or confessed to "taking care of" the cop killer. If he hadn't heard from them by dawn, he was calling them. He wasn't going to let anything stop him from begging them to take him back.

He was exhausted, but every time he closed his eyes, his mind started to replay the worse scenes from his night. And he was sure if he did fall asleep, nightmares would come, ones in which he was shot, or Jack was, or Gray. Shivering, he pulled the blanket tighter around him and stared out into the night. There was no one there to see the tears rolling down his cheeks, but he sat in the dark anyway. Light seemed wrong for the mood he was in.

His eyes drifted closed. Maybe he fell asleep for a second or two, but he jerked awake when he heard a buzz. When he realized what had startled him, he reached for his phone with a shaky hand.

A text from Jack. *Come home.*

Joy coursed through him. Jack was right. When he was with them, he was home.

He fumbled through his reply. *On my way.*

Mason had stripped off his clothes when he got home, thinking he might burn them since they'd always remind him of being at gunpoint and of seeing Ferret Boy take aim at Jack. He'd pulled on a pair of ancient, faded sweats and a threadbare Duke University t-shirt, and he didn't bother to change. He needed to get to Jack and Gray as fast as he could. Once he had shoes on, he ran for the door. Halfway there, he realized he didn't have his keys, and he scrambled around looking for them, cursing every second that he wasn't on the way to his lovers. Finally, he found them on the floor by the bedroom door. They must have fallen out of his pants as he'd kicked them off.

He'd gotten his car fully repaired after he'd broken up with Jack and Gray, thinking he couldn't rely on them to worry about him anymore. And he was very thankful now, because even though they didn't live far from him, biking would have taken far too long. He tried to focus on the road as he drove, but his mind was whirling. Jack and Gray wanted him; they wanted him home with them. Having their arms around him, kissing them, touching them, that's what he needed to feel whole. He'd been so stupid to push them away.

As soon as he put his car in park in their driveway, he jumped out and ran for the door. Jack opened it before Mason could knock. He grabbed Mason and pulled him into his arms. Then Gray was there too, wrapping himself around Mason from behind.

"I've missed you," Mason said against Jack's neck. "I've missed you so much."

"Missed you too." They both squeezed him until he could hardly breathe.

He didn't care, he needed to be held, and he needed to taste them. He kissed the soft flesh of Jack's neck, growing slowly more aggressive until he was biting and sucking and Jack was moaning.

Gray slid his hands under Mason's shirt, caressing him then tweaking his nipples. Mason groaned and sank his teeth into Jack's collarbone.

Jack yelped and Mason grinned as he leaned back against Gray and shifted his attention to Jack's mouth. They kissed, pouring their grief, fear, and desperate need into each other while Gray petted them both. "So sorry," Mason murmured against Jack's lips.

Jack pulled back and cupped his face. "It's okay. I'm sorry too."

"But you—"

"Could have made it clear how I felt, how we both felt."

Gray gripped Mason's shoulders then and turned him around. "You're ours, but we let you walk out the door. We gave up."

Mason shook his head. "No. I ran, and then I refused to admit how fucking scared I was. Today, when I thought…." Mason closed his eyes, fighting back tears.

Jack caressed Mason's cheek with his thumb. "It's okay. We're all okay."

Gray shifted so he could kiss Mason. He licked carefully at the seam of Mason's mouth, and then he brushed his lips against Mason's. Gray's aching tenderness filled Mason with longing for everything he'd thought he'd have to give up. He closed his eyes and savored the sweet contact. And then Jack was there, and they were all three kissing. It was messy and awkward and so fucking perfect.

When they finally stopped to catch their breath, Mason took one of Gray's hands and squeezed it. "I love you." The words came out in a whisper.

Gray's eyes widened. "You do?"

Mason nodded. He reached for Jack, taking one of his hands too. "I love you, too."

Gray smoothed Mason's hair back. "We've loved you for a long time, but we didn't think you...."

"I want this. I've never wanted anything more, but I'm scared. I don't want to come between the two of you."

Gray nodded. "We don't know how to do this either, but we know we need you."

"I need you too."

"Then you're going to have to talk to us. We can't help you if we don't know what's going through your head."

Gray was right, and Mason nodded before he said, "It's not easy for me to need someone. No one's ever really—" His voice broke.

Jack squeezed his hand. "We love you, and we want to take care of you."

"Promise you'll talk to us, that you won't run away again," Gray said, his voice choked with emotion.

Mason glanced at Jack, and he smiled encouragingly. He looked back at Gray, loving that his dark eyes were warm rather than assessing. "I promise I won't run unless it's back here to you."

Gray smiled. "Good. Now can we stop talking and fuck?"

Jack laughed, and Mason did too.

"Come on." Gray steered them down the hall.

They reached for each other as soon as they stepped into the bedroom, and their coming together was frantic and sloppy. They all tried to do everything at once, to touch, to taste, to absorb the other men into them. They were desperate to get closer to each other, and they all stripped as quickly as they could.

Mason needed to feel their skin against every inch of his body. Jack held him close, humping him, their cocks sliding together, the hair on his chest rasping across Mason's smoother skin. Gray pulled them to him and nestled his cock in the crack of Mason's ass. He pumped his hips, letting his hardness slide against Mason's hole.

Mason groaned against Jack's neck, and Jack reached between them, wrapping his hand around both of their cocks and squeezing tightly as he worked them.

Mason was on sensation overload. He couldn't think, couldn't do anything but let the two of them have whatever they wanted from him. He was theirs. How had he ever thought he could walk away from them?

Gray maneuvered them toward the bed, and they all crashed onto the mattress. Jack and Mason arranged themselves with Jack under Mason while Gray got the supplies from the nightstand drawer. Mason forced himself to pull away from Jack long enough to say what he needed to. "Got tested. Wanted to go bare with you, then I ran away and—"

"You mean you'd let me fuck you without this?" Gray held up a condom packet.

Mason nodded. "I trust you."

Jack's eyes widened. "We wanted to ask, but we were afraid of pushing you. Are you sure?"

"I'm sure. I wanted to, so much, but when I got the results, I'd told you I didn't want to see you again."

Jack rubbed his arms. "We're here now. And it's going to be perfect."

"Yes, it is," Gray said as he lubed his fingers.

Jack and Mason kissed and rubbed on each other furiously while Gray prepped Mason's ass. Then Mason pulled away from Jack long enough to gasp out his demand. "Inside me. Now."

Gray scissored his fingers, making Mason cry out. "I need to get you good and ready. I'm not going to be gentle."

"Please!" The word came out louder and more high-pitched than Mason had intended because Jack sank his teeth into Mason's neck, marking him. "Need to know how it feels. Never had bareback."

Gray growled as he pulled his fingers from Mason's body. "I fucking love that I get to be your first." He slapped Mason's ass. "Turn on your side. I want to watch Jack get you both off while I fuck you."

Mason groaned at the thought. He and Jack turned, never releasing each other. Gray lifted Mason's leg, hooking it over Jack's hip, and Jack shifted so he could get a grip on both of their cocks. Gray teased Mason's entrance with the tip of his cock, barely brushing it across the sensitive skin.

"Oh fuck, Gray, just…."

Jack stroked them faster, ending Mason's ability to speak. Then Gray pushed into him without warning, driving forward until his groin brushed Mason's ass. Mason struggled to breathe. The heat of Gray's slick skin was so intense, and just the knowledge that Gray was there with no barrier between them was making him crazy. He squirmed against Gray, wanting him to move. He was so damn full, stretched to the limit, but he was right where he wanted to be.

Jack slowed his strokes, making each one sensual and deliberate. "So good," he whispered.

"Yes." Mason nodded enthusiastically.

Gray growled. He pulled out and pushed back in hard. "Mine."

"Yes," Mason whimpered.

"Mine," Jack said, contorting himself to kiss and bite Mason's chest while still sliding his hand up and down their shafts, matching Gray's rhythm.

Mason moaned and muttered nonsense. He called their names as they speared him between them, thrusting into Jack's hand and pushing back against Gray. He needed them. Wanted them. Wasn't ever going to let them go. "Please. Both. Need you both. Fuck me. Please!"

Gray drove in until his balls slapped Mason's ass, then held still. He circled Jack's wrist with one of his hands, forcing him to stop working his and Mason's cocks. "Do you think you could take us both?"

Mason tried to clear his lust-fogged brain. "W-what?"

"Would you like it if we both fucked you at the same time?"

"You mean…."

Gray chuckled. "I mean both our cocks in you at the same time, stretching you until you screamed."

"Oh my God!" Mason almost came just from the thought.

"You think you could take it?"

"I…I don't…can't think…can't…"

Panic and need and overwhelming sensation had Mason tipping his head back onto Gray's shoulder and shaking it back and forth. He couldn't form words, couldn't think.

"When we've got more patience to get you ready, to drive you so insane you're begging for us, we'll show you what it means to really belong to both of us. You want that, don't you?"

"Yes." Mason finally made his voice work.

"Good." Gray's voice was low and sexy, and the word vibrated through Mason.

Gray pulled out just a little then drove back in. "I want you to be so full you can't take anything else, anyone else."

"No one else. Just you and Jack. Always," Mason gasped. Once again, he'd let something slip

that he shouldn't have. But this time he didn't
panic. He'd promised he wouldn't run from what he
felt. And neither Jack nor Gray had reacted to what
he'd said with anything but groans and faster
fucking.

Gray slid one of his hands into Mason's hair
and tugged his head back hard enough to make
Mason cry out. He squeezed Mason's hip with his
other hand, gripping hard and holding him in place.
Then he pulled out with agonizing slowness. "I
want you to feel every inch of me. I want you to
know you're mine."

"Yes. God yes."

Jack worked Mason's cock harder as Gray
pushed slowly into Mason inch by inch. The slow
fucking didn't last long though. Soon he was back
to taking Mason with a punishing rhythm.

Mason shouted. "Can't last. Please. Got to
come. Now."

"Do it," Gray growled.

Gray's words sent Mason over the edge. His
orgasm slammed through him, and he didn't know
if his scream kept echoing in his head or if he really
yelled over and over as he pumped out his seed,
coating Jack's hand, slicking the way for him.

Jack shuddered, and Mason pulled him closer
and slid a hand between them. He pumped Jack,
once, twice. Jack drove himself into Mason's hand
and tensed. Warmth flowed over Mason's fingers as
Jack shot his load, crying Mason's name.

Gray thrust into Mason in short, harsh strokes
as he grunted and came, fingers digging into
Mason's hip to keep him tight against Gray's body.

Mason gasped at the sensation of Gray's hot come flooding his ass, marking him.

By the time Gray's cock slipped from his ass, Mason was barely awake. He whimpered at the loss of Gray's warmth when the big man rolled over and stood. "Be right back," he grunted.

Mason was a sticky, sweaty mess, and Jack was too, but Mason didn't care. He couldn't possibly move.

Gray returned and knelt on the bed. Mason smiled up at him as Gray used a warm washcloth to clean him up. Then Gray pulled the cover over him and concentrated on cleaning Jack. Mason heard them kiss, and he snuggled over against Jack while Gray took the washcloths back to the bathroom.

Gray returned to bed a few seconds later. He slid under the covers and wrapped his big body around Mason. Mason reveled in the comfort of being in both their arms. He'd never felt more at home in his life.

Chapter Sixteen

Mason was disoriented when he woke the next morning. When he realized where he was, his heart started to pound, because Jack and Gray weren't in bed with him. He didn't want them to have left before he could talk to them. But the rattle of pans from down the hall let him know Jack was making breakfast.

Mason glanced at the clock. Seven AM. At most, he'd had three hours of sleep, but he didn't want to stay in bed without his lovers. So he kicked off the covers and stumbled into the bathroom where he showered as quickly as his still-asleep brain could manage. Then, slightly embarrassed, he pulled on his ragged t-shirt and sweats that he'd refused to change out of in his haste to get there.

When he walked into the kitchen, Gray and Jack were leaning against the counter, frowning at something on the computer. They were both in uniform, and their pants hugged their perfect asses. Mason gave a low whistle.

Gray looked up, and his expression changed instantly, a grin replacing his scowl. "Good morning."

Being able to put such happiness on Gray's face warmed Mason all the way down to his toes.

"Coffee?" Jack asked.

Mason nodded. "Please."

Jack closed his laptop and stood. "I'll get it."

"Is everything okay?" Mason asked.

Jack sighed. "Yeah, the fucking paper got just about everything wrong in the article about last night's robberies."

"There was more than one?"

Gray responded. "Yeah, apparently, Davis—"

"Is that the man who was with Gwen?"

"Yes. Apparently, he and two other men robbed Sayer's before Davis came to Nathan's to meet up with Gwen. She was supposed to already have the money in hand so they could make a quick getaway."

"Did the police find the other men?"

Jack nodded as he handed Mason a steaming mug of coffee. "They were caught before Gray and I got to Nathan's."

"Is that everyone who was involved or are you still looking for some of them?" Mason asked, hoping the answer was the one he wanted to hear.

"That's all as best we can tell. Davis was fairly quick to rat out his partners. I think if there were more he would have told us," Jack said.

Mason let out the breath he'd been holding. He wouldn't have to worry about another of their conspirators coming after him. "So the paper got it all wrong. That sounds typical," he said.

Jack snorted. "Sadly, it is."

Gray looked angrier. "They're making us look like idiots for taking so long to catch them. We had some great leads but no solid evidence. We could have stopped them sooner if we hadn't done things by the book, but then we'd catch hell for that. Do they think we wanted Ronnie to die? Do they think we wouldn't have prevented it if we could have?" He slammed his hand down on the counter.

Mason set his cup down and wrapped his arms around Gray, wanting to soothe him.

Jack laid a hand on Gray's arm. "They get things wrong all the time, Gray; it's okay."

He nodded, but Mason could feel the tension in his back muscles as he pulled him closer. Then suddenly, Gray deflated, sagging against the counter. "I can't take this anymore."

"People not understanding how hard you work?"

He shook his head. "That's just…it pisses me off, but…."

"Then what's wrong?" Mason asked.

"I'm sick of hiding."

Jack's coffee mug started to slip from his hand. He caught it just as it was about to hit the floor. Coffee sloshed out, but he didn't even look at it. He stared at Gray, and Mason couldn't tell if he was angry or just shocked.

"I'm tired of pretending I'm straight, of pretending we're only partners at work, of pretending Mason is just a friend. I…I just don't know if I can do it anymore."

Jack set his cup down very deliberately. Mason was more concerned by the icy calm he was radiating than he'd ever been by Gray's anger. "When I tried to talk to you about this months ago—"

"Ron hadn't been killed. We hadn't met Mason. I hadn't been threatened."

"Threatened?" Mason looked at him. "Who would threaten you?" Mason assumed most people were as intimidated by Gray as he would have been if Gray hadn't started flirting with him the first time they met.

"Someone who's decided he knows the truth."

Jack snarled. "One of the fucking homophobes at work saw Gray hug me. I'd had a bad day. There wasn't anything inappropriate about it. I've hugged co-workers plenty of times, but he already suspected what was up between us, and when he saw it, he took it as confirmation." Jack shook his head. "Maybe I did let some emotion slip. I was about to fall apart and I needed Gray."

"And you shouldn't have to be ashamed of that."

Jack's expression hardened again. "We shouldn't have to hide the fact that we're gay, but our captain is never going to let a couple be partnered. They wouldn't do that for a het couple either. If we come out, they'll reassign one of us to another precinct."

Mason wanted to be able to comfort them, but he didn't know what to say. "You don't think they'll just give you each a new partner?"

Jack shook his head. "No, they'll say we're going to compromise investigations if we work together, even if we're not partnered."

Gray pushed away from the counter and turned to look at Jack. "We damn near fucked up this one."

Mason realized then why Gray was taking the article in the paper so hard. He was beating himself up for losing control with Davis.

The color drained from Jack's face. "Are you saying we shouldn't work together?"

Gray looked down. "I thought the fucker was going to shoot you, Jack, or shoot Mason. I didn't know Mason would be able to…I thought…." He squeezed his eyes shut and balled his hands into fists.

"You were angry and you overreacted," Jack said, but he didn't sound convinced.

"I overreacted because it was you, you and Mason."

Jack moved until he was right in front of Gray. He took Gray's hands in his, making him open his fists so Jack could hold onto him.

"It's going to be okay. We'll figure out what to do."

After a few long, silent seconds, Gray nodded. "I'm sorry."

Jack shook his head. "Don't bc. I…I've been avoiding this. We need to talk about it."

Gray nodded. "Maybe we can talk tonight after we show Mason how it feels to have both of us inside him."

Jack smiled then and both men looked at Mason. He swallowed hard. He hadn't been sure they would remember. They'd all been so crazed when they were fucking. "Um…you really want to try that?"

Gray raised a brow. "Want to? Hell yeah, we want to."

Jack laughed, and Mason was glad to see him happy again even if there were some very hard decisions they were going to have to make very soon.

"We've wanted to since the first night we were together, but we didn't want to scare you," Jack said.

Mason chewed on his bottom lip. The thought of taking them both had his cock half hard already, but part of him was also more than a little afraid. "Um…I'm just…."

Gray reached for him and then both men pulled him into a three-way hug.

"We'll take good care of you," Jack said. "Don't worry."

Mason nodded, and his mind started to spin out a fantasy. They would tie him up, tease him, make him beg to have them both. In his vision, both his men were in uniform, belts hanging low on their hips, cuffs dangling from their sides. Mason suppressed a shudder. He really had developed a cop fetish.

"Would you…." Mason's cheeks heated, and he wasn't sure he could finish his request.

"Would we what?" Jack asked, grinning like he knew it was something dirty.

Mason licked his lips and swallowed. "Would you wear your uniforms tonight?"

"When we stuff you full of both our cocks?" Gray asked.

Mason sucked in his breath. His cock swelled more, and he nodded, sure no words would come out.

Gray glared at him.

At first he was afraid he'd said something wrong, then he realized what Gray wanted, and he found a way to make his voice work. "Yes, sir."

Gray smiled then, genuine happiness lighting up his face. "We're going to make tonight very special for you."

His words made Mason's chest tighten. "I love you, both of you."

Jack laid a hand on the small of Mason's back, and Gray cupped his chin and tilted his head so he was looking up. Then he brushed his lips across Mason's. "I love you too."

Mason tried to pull Gray in for a deeper kiss, but he stepped back. "No more. I want you thinking about us all day. I want you so frazzled you can't concentrate because you're so eager to have us both."

"Gray—"

"And don't even think about jerking off. I want you worried you're going to come in your pants."

Jack groaned, and Mason looked over at him. He was rubbing his cock through his uniform pants. "Jesus, Gray! How are *we* supposed to work?"

"Hands off," Gray commanded. "You're just going to have to deal with the anticipation."

Jack frowned, but he did as he was told. "This is going to be a long damn day."

Gray grinned. "Yeah, but it's going to be worth it."

Jack nodded in agreement as he grabbed their hats off the counter. "We've got to get going."

"Let me grab my keys so you can lock up," Mason said.

Gray shook his head. "You don't need to go now."

Jack lifted a key off the rack by the door and handed it to Mason. "This is yours."

Mason stared at the small silver object in his hand as if he couldn't quite comprehend what it was and what it meant. Finally, he looked up at Jack. "You don't mind if I stay here?"

"We want you to stay. And not just until you need to go to work."

"We'd like you to move in," Gray said.

Mason simply stared at them. First Gray announced that he wanted to be out at work and then they asked him to move in. This was way too much to process after a night of very little sleep. "M-Move in? But you…but we…."

Gray glanced at the clock. "Fuck! We're going to be late, and considering that I may be about to be suspended, I'd better at least show up on time."

Jack nodded. "Think about it, Mason. We'll talk tonight."

They rushed out the door, leaving Mason standing there, holding his new key and realizing he wanted to be there with them every night *and* every morning, no matter how crazy that sounded.

Chapter Seventeen

A few hours after Jack and Gray left for work, Elizabeth called and let Mason know the police had still not given her the go-ahead to reopen. She expected to be open by dinner though, and she wanted him to come in and help with inventory and clean up.

Mason was thankful she needed him. Otherwise, he would have sat around alternately being nervous about what Jack and Gray had planned for him and fighting the urge to jerk off to his fantasies about the evening. At least the anticipation was helping him not think about how close he'd come to getting shot and possibly killed the day before.

When he walked into Nathan's, his heart rate accelerated, and he found it hard to breathe. But he made himself keep walking, right over to the bar where Elizabeth was talking to Detective Marsh. Rather than stopping the images that came to mind of what had happened, he let himself replay the night in his mind. By the time the flood of memories stopped, his hands were sweaty and he was breathing hard.

Elizabeth glanced his way and her eyes widened. "Are you okay?"

He nodded. "Yeah, I will be anyway. I just have to get used to being here again after…."

"If you need more time—"

"No!" The word came out harsher than he meant it. He ran a hand through his hair. "I'm sorry. I have to face it. I'm not going to let them force me to stay away."

Detective Marsh nodded in agreement. "That's good. But if you need to talk to someone about what happened, let me know. I'll put you in touch with a good therapist."

"Thanks," Mason said. He appreciated the concern, but he much preferred the type of therapy Jack and Gray had planned. Comfort and hard fucking from his men was all he needed to give him the strength to face his fears, or at least, he hoped so.

They were able to open Nathan's in the late afternoon. By then Mason had managed to work in the office with Elizabeth for several hours without freaking out. Before he got behind the bar and started serving, he forced himself to walk into the kitchen and stand where he'd been when Davis, aka Ferret Boy, had pulled his gun on Mason.

Pure terror raced through him, but he stood his ground. Gwen and the assholes she worked with weren't going to keep him from doing his job. And as soon as he finished for the night, he would go home to Jack and Gray.

At least the horror of being held at gunpoint forced him to see what an idiot he'd been about his relationship with Jack and Gray. He loved them, and no matter how crazy that was, no matter that for now they had to hide it, he was going to do everything he could to keep them all together. What he hadn't realized before was that Jack and Gray needed him just like he needed them. He wasn't going to let them down.

Elizabeth stayed until closing and Anderson, one of the officers who'd been with Jack and Gray the day before, stopped by to make sure everything was secure and to escort Elizabeth and Mason to their cars. The police believed they'd caught everyone involved, but they were still being cautious, and Mason was thankful for that.

"So you're good friends with Jack and Gray," Anderson asked as he walked Mason out.

Mason's heart thudded against his chest. Surely his being their friend wasn't a problem, was it? "Yeah, I got to know them working here."

"That's cool. They haven't been hanging out with the guys from work much lately; I hope they're doing okay."

Mason nodded. "They seem to be."

"Good. Well, have a good night."

"You too."

Mason shut his car door and started the engine. He wondered if Anderson was just being friendly or if he was digging for information. Did he suspect that Jack and Gray were partners outside of work? He was almost certain Detective Marsh knew what was going on, but if he were going to say something, he would have done it already.

Thoughts of Jack and Gray's fellow officers left Mason quickly as he drove out of downtown. By the time he pulled up in front of their house a few minutes later, his cock was hard as steel. He jumped out, beeped the car locked, and headed to the porch.

He knocked, but no one answered. Both their cars were in the driveway, one behind the other. He started to knock again, then remembered he had a key so he unlocked the door and stepped inside.

Immediately the light went on. Jack was standing right in front of him. "What are you doing back here?"

Gray shut the door and crowded behind him. "You planning to rob a cop? I thought you were smarter than that."

Mason glanced from one of them to the other. They were both in uniforms as promised and the sight of them made him want to strip and offer himself right there, but he knew it would be better if he played along. "You've got it all wrong, officer. I came back because I didn't get enough of you the last time."

Jack laughed. "You're a slutty little thing, aren't you?"

"Only for you," he winked at Jack.

"Get on your knees," Jack said, as he began undoing his belt.

Mason did as he was asked. Jack handed his belt to Gray, who put it on the table by the door. Mason had noticed that neither of them had their guns. They liked to play safe anyway, but he was sure they were also thinking about him and wanting him to be comfortable. He was lucky to have such considerate men in his life.

Jack undid his pants, and Mason reached inside to free his cock. He slid his hand up and down

Jack's length before flicking his tongue across the tip and eliciting a hiss from him. As Mason leaned forward, ready to draw Jack into his mouth, he glanced at Gray, who now stood beside Jack. He was staring at Mason, eyes wide, chest rising and falling.

"Come on," Jack urged. "Take it into your mouth. Show me what you can do."

Mason sucked him then, bobbing his head rapidly while he worked the base of Jack's shaft with his hand. As Jack's moans and incomprehensible words grew more frenetic, Mason took him deeper until he had Jack's full length down his throat.

"Holy fuck!" Gray's shout made Mason smile around Jack's length. He loved when he got Gray that stirred up.

Jack grabbed his head then and took control, fucking his mouth with short, fast strokes. Mason relaxed and let Jack use him the way he wanted to. Out of the corner of his eye, he saw Gray pull something from his belt. When he realized it was a nightstick, he almost choked himself on Jack's dick.

Gray caressed it, his fingers moving up and down the long, thick shaft. He stepped behind Mason and laid the tip of the stick between his shoulder blades. With firm pressure, he slid it down the length of Mason's spine.

Mason arched into the touch, sputtering as Gray distracted him from sucking Jack.

Gray kept going, dragging the deliciously phallic-shaped stick along the crack of his ass, then pushing it between his legs. When he pressed the tip against Mason's balls, Mason groaned around Jack's cock and started sucking him harder. The pressure felt so good, even through his clothes. He needed Jack to come so he could get Gray to stop teasing him.

Gray pressed the stick against him harder. Mason pushed back against it, wanting more.

Gray groaned. "Fuck, you'd look hot with my stick up your ass."

Mason whimpered around Jack's dick and worked himself against the nightstick.

Gray laughed and let the stick fall to the floor with thump. Mason heard him undoing his belt. He let the rest of his police paraphernalia hit the floor and walked around Mason until he stood beside Jack again. Then he unfastened his pants and pulled his cock out. "Suck both of us," he said, his voice gruff with need. The sight of them with their uniforms on and their cocks hanging out was nasty and hot, like the best cop porn ever.

Mason wrapped a hand around Gray's cock as he continued to suck Jack. Then he shifted his attention to Gray's, loving their mingled taste. He moved back and forth between them until they were both panting and thrusting into his mouth as he sucked them. He was dizzy with the power of stimulating them both while his submissive side loved being on his knees, serving them, doing exactly what they told him to do.

He slid his hand along Jack's length, glancing up to see his eyes shut, his mouth hanging open. He leaned over to Gray, ready to take him into his mouth again, but Gray stepped back.

"Don't make him stop," Jack pleaded.

"When we come, we're going to be inside him." Gray's tone made it clear that arguing would be futile.

Jack gasped when Mason gave a final firm tug on his cock then sat back on his heels.

Gray smiled down at him. "You ever had two cocks inside you at the same time, boy?"

Mason shook his head frantically, his heart thundering against his chest.

Gray chuckled. "He looks a little scared."

Jack shook his head and grinned, stroking his cock absently. "I would be too if both of these were going up my ass."

Mason's chest tightened. He could barely breathe. He wanted what they offered, but he was more than a little nervous.

"Bedroom. Now." Gray gestured down the hall.

Mason stood, but he wasn't sure his legs would hold him up. He managed to stumble to the bedroom, but he had to grip the doorframe to steady himself. When he heard Gray's heavy footsteps behind him followed by Jack's faster, lighter ones, he wobbled into the bedroom and waited, holding his breath to see what Gray would tell him to do next.

But it was Jack who laid a hand against the small of his back and told him what to do. "Take your clothes off and get on the bed."

Mason pulled his t-shirt over his head then struggled to make his fingers co-operate to unfasten his jeans. Finally he got them loose and pushed them over his hips, but he nearly fell down trying to toe off his shoes. When he lay down and turned to face Jack and Gray, they were both staring at him with predatory looks on their faces.

"Did you bring the cuffs?" Gray asked Jack.

"Oh yeah." Jack gave Mason an evil grin. Then he crawled up on the bed. "Put your hands over your head."

Mason reached up and gripped the headboard. Jack slid the cuffs around one of the slats in the headboard, then snapped one around each of Mason's wrists. They weren't the police-issue cuffs normally on their belts. They were lined with soft material made for the kind of play they all enjoyed.

Gray laid a hand on Mason's thigh. "Open wider."

Mason shivered as he complied, dropping his legs open so Gray had perfect access. Jack handed Gray a tube of lube, and he slicked up the fingers of his right hand, all four of them. Mason's eyes widened.

"I've got to open you up good if you're going to take both of us up there."

Mason nodded slowly, hoping Gray didn't insist he answer. Gray must have known he was overwhelmed, because he caressed the inside of his thigh and didn't push further, not for his obedience anyway. He did push a finger in all the way to the knuckle, making Mason gasp and arch up to meet him.

"Eager, aren't you, boy?"

"Y-yes," Mason cried out as Jack pinched one of his nipples, then used his tongue to ease the sting.

Gray eased in and out of his ass while Jack continued to torment his nipples.

"You like this, boy?" Gray asked.

Mason nodded frantically.

Gray teased the edge of his entrance with another finger. "Answer properly if you want more."

"Yes, sir. I…oh God." Gray added a second finger and drove deep enough to brush Mason's prostate. "More please, sir."

Gray slid out and added a third finger.

Mason sank his teeth into his lower lip. The stretch was almost too much, but it felt so damn good at the same time. He wanted to be full, so full he forgot everything but Jack and Gray.

He whimpered when Gray pulled his digits out. "Does that hurt, boy?"

"Yes. No. I…"

"Suck him, Jack," Gray ordered.

"With pleasure." Jack leaned over and gripped Mason's cock, angling it toward his mouth. He looked up at Mason as he swallowed him down. Mason bucked up into his mouth, but Jack shoved his hips back to the mattress. "Stay still."

"Can't." He squirmed, trying to get loose.

Gray slapped his ass. "Don't make us tell you again."

Mason squeezed his eyes shut and concentrated on keeping his hips still, but between Jack's hot mouth and Gray's thick fingers he was sure he was going to lose his mind. Jack sucked him hard, and Gray drove into him faster and faster.

"Please!"

"Take it," Gray growled.

Mason tried but he couldn't stay still. Jack held him down, and Mason started jerking on the cuffs. "Have to touch you. Please!"

Suddenly panic hit him. He needed to be free. He needed Jack and Gray, not the men they were pretending to be, but the real men who loved him.

"Please!" He was so far gone with the twisted up feelings of fear and pleasure that he couldn't think what to say. Then he remembered his safeword. Red. But before he uttered it, Gray realized something was truly wrong.

"Stop, Jack," he shouted.

Jack released Mason's cock and sat back on his heels, but he kept a hand on Mason's stomach, caressing him with soothing strokes.

Gray slipped his slick fingers from Mason's ass. "What's wrong?"

Mason wanted to explain, but he needed to touch them first. He tried to reach for them and remembered he was still cuffed.

Gray looked at Jack. "Uncuff him."

Jack released his wrists and Mason reached for him, pulling him down until their lips were about an inch apart. "Kiss me," he whispered, sounding incredibly vulnerable.

Jack reverently brushed his lips over Mason's. "I love you."

Mason blinked back the hot tears that had risen to his eyes. "I love you too."

He looked up at Gray then, hating the worry on his face. "I love you both, and I do want this, but I want it to be just us, no games, just us like we really are."

Gray shifted so he could touch Mason's face. He caressed Mason's cheek as he spoke. "Then that's exactly how we'll do it."

Chapter Eighteen

Jack started unbuttoning his shirt, and Mason frowned at him.

Jack raised a brow. "What?"

Mason looked from one man to another. "Um…I know I said no games, but you're just so fucking sexy in your uniforms, and it makes what we're doing…I don't know…nastier."

Jack laughed, stopped working on his shirt, and kissed Mason instead. Gray pushed his fingers back into Mason suddenly, making Mason gasp. But within seconds, he was bearing down, trying to get them deeper, nearly out of his head with want. He wrapped a hand around the back of Jack's neck, holding him still so he could get a good taste. When he finally let go so he could get some air, Jack walked on his knees until he was beside Gray.

Mason reached for him, but Jack shook his head. "I want to watch him get you ready. I want to see all his fingers disappear into you."

Mason made a strangled noise. Gray looked at Jack, and they smiled at each other. Then Gray pulled all the way out and pushed back in with all four fingers.

"Oh my fucking God," Mason yelled. "Are you…I can't…."

Gray held his hand still. Only the tip of his pinkie was inside Mason.

Mason tried to get a breath. He needed to know if Gray was going to try to put his whole hand up his ass. All he got out was "G-gray?"

Gray smiled at him, rubbing his abdomen with his free hand. "It's okay, I won't go any further than my fingers tonight."

Tonight? "Okay, I don't know if I can—"

Gray laid a finger over his lips. "It's fine. You don't have to want more, ever. If you do, we'll take it very slowly."

Mason nodded. He would never have thought he'd want a man to fist him, but now, with Gray's four fingers in him, he wasn't sure there was anything he wouldn't want from Gray.

Gray pushed in a little farther and Mason groaned.

"Is this okay?" Gray asked.

Mason nodded.

Gray went deeper.

Mason gasped and shook his head. "Can't."

Gray pulled back, just enough to ease the pressure until it was bearable. "Do you want me to stop?"

Do I? Fuck, Mason didn't know. He was scared, but this was Gray who was stretching him. Gray would be careful. "No."

Jack wrapped a hand around Mason's cock and starting jerking him off, working him until he was more concerned with pushing up into Jack's hand than with the ache in his ass. As he relaxed, Gray was able to push in more. It felt incredible to be so full. Just the idea of all of Gray's fingers inside him to the knuckle drove him to the brink of climax, and he welcomed the burn as Jack's hand moved faster on his cock. "More," he begged. "Fuck me with your hand."

Gray gave him what he wanted, and in seconds Mason was squirming, pushing against Gray, trying to take even more, but Gray pulled back. "That's enough for now."

Mason knew he was right, but he still protested when Gray released him.

"Get me ready," Gray said, stretching out on his back next to Mason.

Jack handed Mason the lube. Mason squirted some in his hand and slicked up Gray's cock. Then Jack took the bottle from him so he could get himself ready.

As Mason slid his hand slid up and down Gray's fat length, he became mesmerized thinking about Gray buried inside him with Jack there too, both their cocks bare, rubbing against each other inside his ass. His own cock was painfully hard and his ass fluttered, feeling much too empty after being stretched so far by Gray's hand.

"Ride me," Gray commanded.

Mason straddled him and gripped Gray's dick so he could line it up. Then he sank down slowly, letting Gray's cock open him back up. "Feels so damn good."

"God, yes. So hot having you like this, with nothing between us." Gray suddenly tensed.

"You ok?" Mason asked.

He gave Mason a strained smile. "Yeah. Just trying not to lose it before Jack can join me."

His words made Mason's cock jerk, and his ass tightened around Gray.

"Fuck," Gray roared. "That's not helping."

"Sorry." Mason grinned, but he wasn't really sorry—and Gray knew it.

Mason rose and fell, loving the feel of Gray's entire length buried in him. Then Jack laid a hand on his back, pushing him forward. "My turn."

Mason moaned when Jack teased the edge of his entrance with the tip of his cock. Gray wrapped his arms around Mason and pulled him down until he lay on Gray's chest. Jack teased a little more, then he started to push inside. Mason tensed. This was going to hurt.

"Relax." Gray stroked. "I've got you."

Mason tried to breathe and sink into Gray, but when Jack pushed in more, Mason cried out, certain he was being split in two.

Gray reached between them and circled Mason's cock. Mason raised up enough for Gray to be able to give him tight, firm strokes.

Jack eased forward again. Pleasure, pain. Too much and not enough.

"Don't stop," Mason pleaded. It hurt but somehow it felt so fucking perfect to have them both.

"I won't." Jack pushed deeper.

Mason bit his lip, holding in a sob.

"Let it out and stop us if it's too much," Gray scolded. "We can try another time or never. We want you to enjoy this."

"I do. I need this, I just…."

Gray stroked his cock harder, and Jack licked and nibbled his neck, his shoulders, his back. Then he bit down on the curve of Mason's neck and drove in the rest of the way.

Gray teased the slit and stroked him in his favorite way. Mason screamed as pain combined with the pleasure. It was too much, both physically and emotionally. Mason thought he might combust. "Oh god, we're really…you two are really…."

"Yes!" Jack shouted. He pulled back and thrust in farther.

Mason had never imagined he could be so full and not break. Full of cock. Full of need. Full of love.

"Love this," Gray said. "Feeling Jack's cock on mine, taking you like this, possessing you, owning you."

"Yes!" Mason yelled. He bucked wildly between them, trying to get them to move. "Fuck me. Stop going slow and fuck me."

Jack made a strangled noise and did just that. Gray held tight to Mason and shoved his hips upward as much as he could.

Mason was panting, crazed with need. He couldn't believe how amazing it felt when his body adjusted to having them both. He opened his eyes and looked down at Gray. The ecstasy on his face nearly sent Mason over the edge. "Must feel so good," he said. "Jack's cock on yours."

Gray growled. "We'll take Jack together and you'll see. It's unbelievable. So tight. So hot."

Mason squeezed his eyes shut and fought the urge to come. The thought of him and Gray taking

Jack like this, having him speared between them....
"So hot. So good."

"Yes!" Jack shouted. He pushed in hard,
pressing Gray's cock against Mason's gland.

Mason's balls tightened. "So close," he panted.

"Me too," Jack said. "Can't last. Oh. My.
God." Jack shouted and went wild, driving into
Mason in harsh bursts.

Mason writhed between his lovers, his cock
rubbing against Gray's abdomen. He was going to
go up in flames, to die, to break in half, but he knew
his men would put him back together. "Yours!" He
screamed it. "Yours, oh yes!" Words turned to
crazed animal sounds as his orgasm slammed
through him.

Gray held Mason's hips and pumped upward,
impaling him. Then Gray roared and jerked against
Mason just as the world started to fade to black.

When Mason came to awareness again, he was
still sprawled on top of Gray, but Jack was beside
them stroking Mason's back, his leg thrown over
Mason's and Gray's.

"Am I still alive?" Mason asked.

Jack laughed. "I think so."

"Don't ask me to get up anytime soon," Gray
said.

Mason felt the rumble of Gray's voice in his
chest. "That was...."

When Mason didn't finish his sentence, Jack
smiled indulgently. "Indescribable?"

"Yeah," Mason agreed. Mason could feel their
cum sliding from his body, dampening his thighs.
His ass ached, but it was so worth it.

Gray hooked a finger under his chin and encouraged him to look up. "Are you okay?"

"I…" Mason paused. It was a good thing he wouldn't have to sit much the next day, but otherwise he was fine, more than fine. For the first time, he believed that he and Jack and Gray had a real chance at making a three-way relationship work.

"I'm wonderful."

"We didn't hurt you?" Jack asked, caressing his ass.

"I won't stop feeling this for a while, but that's not a bad thing."

"Are you sure?" Gray asked.

"Yeah, I kinda like that."

Jack grinned. "He's like me, Gray. He fucking loves feeling it all day."

"Might be more than a day this time," Mason said.

Gray looked worried again.

Jack sighed. "That's even better. When it's been really good, when you've let go and surrendered to what you want, that's when you don't stop feeling it for a long time, physically or here." Jack laid a hand over his heart. "Gray, you never take things further than either of us want."

Mason cupped Gray's face. "I love you. And I love what you do to me. I know I can trust you."

"You didn't before."

Mason frowned. "I've always known you wouldn't hurt me. I wasn't even scared the night you 'arrested' me at the bar."

"You trusted me not to take you beyond what you wanted physically, but you didn't trust me not to hurt you here." He laid his hand on Mason's chest, mimicking Jack's gesture.

Tears pricked the back of Mason's eyes. He didn't know what to say. Gray was right, but he knew better now.

Jack laid a hand on both their shoulders. "That kind of trust is much harder to come by, but we've all learned what we need."

Mason nodded. "He's right. I trust you both now. I love you, and I want this to work."

"I want this to work too, and I don't want to hide it," Gray said.

Jack kissed each of them then, a sweet, soft brush of his lips. "Let's not rush into things. We have options. None of them seem perfect right now, but as long as we all love each other, and we're all willing to forget about how crazy the idea of the three of us together is and accept what we know we need, we'll find a way."

Mason agreed. "Yeah, we will."

Gray smiled. "I love you both."

Jack pulled both men to him and held them tight. Mason's chest ached with love for them, with concern for his lovers' future, with the thought of how they walked into danger every day, but Jack was right. They had to take this slowly, and for right now, he had them both, their arms around him, the heat of their bodies pressed together.

He kissed each of them. Then they all dove into a messy three-way kiss that had them groaning and laughing at the same time. Mason knew that as long as they could make each other laugh and smile, they were going to be just fine.

The End

Author Bio

Silvia Violet writes erotic romance and erotica in a variety of genres including sci fi, paranormal and historical. She can be found haunting coffee shops looking for the darkest, strongest cup of coffee she can find. Once equipped with the needed fuel, she can happily sit for hours pounding away at her laptop. Silvia typically leaves home disguised as a suburban stay-at-home-mom, and other coffee shop patrons tend to ask her hilarious questions like "Do you write children's books?" She loves watching the looks on their faces when they learn what she's actually up to.

When not writing, Silvia enjoys baking sinful chocolate treats, exploring new styles of cooking, and reading children's books to her wickedly smart offspring. You can get to know Silvia better by visiting her blog or finding her on Facebook.

Website: http://silviaviolet.com

Facebook: http://facebook.com/silvia.violet

Silvia Violet

Twitter: http://twitter.com/Silvia_Violet

For a list of Silvia's available titles:
http://silviaviolet.com/books

Fitting In

Discover the men of Silvia Violet's *Wild R Farm.*

Here's a sneak peek from *Wild R Farm 1: Finding Release.*

"That should be the last of it." Jonah tossed the final sack of feed on the back of Cole's truck parked outside his family's feed store. "You need anything else?"

Jonah looked at Cole with his big brown eyes as if he needed something. Cole caught his scent, and his wolf stirred to life. He smelled like horse and sweat with an underlying citrusy scent, young and clean. Prey. Cole's cock wanted to fulfill all Jonah's needs, but Cole wasn't stupid enough to even flirt with an eighteen-year-old high school senior whose stepfather had been the most vocally anti-gay preacher in town. The only reason the Marks family deigned to sell him grain was because in these hard times they needed his money.

Cole tried to ignore the fantasies playing out in his mind. "Nope. We're good."

Jonah looked down at his dusty boots. "You got a minute?"

Cole took a deep breath. He glanced around. They couldn't talk here, not openly. Jonah needed a friend, and Cole had once been young and different and scared. "Sure. You wanna get a cup of coffee?" He tilted his head toward the diner down the street.

"Yeah." Jonah looked at his watch. "I'm due for a break."

"All right. Mind if I leave the truck here?" Cole asked.

"Nah, we're not expecting another big delivery until this afternoon."

They walked to the diner in awkward silence.

Cole couldn't let himself think about how gorgeous Jonah looked, staring at him with those puppy dog eyes. Jonah was off limits for too many reasons to count.

They got a booth by the front windows, and Cole ordered coffee for them. Once the waitress brought the steaming mugs, Cole let himself look at Jonah. His red-brown hair was rumpled from finger combing. A combination of sunburn and embarrassment tinted his cheeks. His denim jacket hugged his broad shoulders and… No! Cole wasn't going to let his perusal go any lower, not even in his imagination. His wolf growled deep inside, his werewolf nature recognizing the equine inside Jonah, the shifter side his family forced him to deny.

He concentrated on Jonah's strong, pale hands as they wrapped around the coffee cup, holding it tight for warmth and stability. Cole wanted to reach out and take Jonah's hands in his own, but that would be bad for both of them.

Cole realized he'd made a mistake. He should have told Jonah he was in a hurry to get back to the farm, or something that would've kept him from sitting here alone with a very young horse shifter who was having an indescribable effect on him.

"Mr Wilder?"

Well, being addressed as 'Mister' certainly burst the lurid fantasy in his mind. He was only thirty, but now he felt ancient. "You know you can call me Cole."

Jonah's cheeks got even redder. "I know… it's just… I was wondering if you'd consider hiring me. I know I don't have experience working in a barn, but, I… well… I'm kind of a natural with horses." He grinned as he said this.

His cutely upturned mouth made him look even younger, and Cole cursed his inappropriate thoughts. The boy needed his help, not his perving.

Jonah's home life had to be hell. His father had left them when he was little, and his mother and elder brother were both self-righteous Bible-thumpers. From what he could tell, Jonah couldn't do a damn thing right in their eyes, but Jonah working at Wild R Farm would be a disaster. Cole could smell Jonah's desire for him. Sooner or later, he'd give into his own desire and exploit that. Jonah deserved freedom and a man who had more self-control.

Cole's wolf growled, the sound almost escaping Cole's mouth. If he put his hands on Jonah, he feared his wolfish instincts would take over. Jonah smelled like prey, like something to be consumed, possessed. Cole shuddered. No. He could never let those desires loose. "Jonah, I—"

"Please…" He dropped his voice to a whisper. "My family… I can't live with them anymore."

"Your mother's not going to let you work for me."

"I'm eighteen. She can't stop me."

Cole tried a different tactic. "You need to finish school. Didn't I hear you'd won a scholarship?"

Jonah looked directly into Cole's eyes as if willing him to understand. "Yeah, but I can't take it anymore."

"You'll graduate in four months. Then you can get out of here, go to college."

He shook his head. "I won't last that long."

He wouldn't last long on Cole's farm either, if Cole snapped and let his werewolf side take control. "Why ask me?" Cole thought he knew, but he wanted confirmation.

Jonah glanced around the restaurant. Only a few tables were occupied, and no one sat nearby. In a voice so low even Cole's sensitive ears could barely hear, he said "Cole, I'm… different, like you. If my brother finds out…"

If Nathan found out, he'd kick Jonah out, maybe beat him. Cole wished Jonah didn't stir him up so much. "I'm sorry. I've got all the hands I need right now."

The eager light went out of Jonah's eyes. He sloshed coffee on the table in his haste to get out of the booth. "OK, I understand. I'm sorry."

Cole grabbed Jonah's arm before he could run. Heat snapped between them, nearly making Cole let go. "I'm sorry for what you're going through."

Jonah shook his head. "Not sorry enough." He pulled free and left.

Jonah's condemnation hit Cole like a punch to the gut. Cole leaned back and closed his eyes, willing the thick, bitter coffee to stay down.

Wild R Farm Book 2: Arresting Love is available now.
Look for *Wild R Farm 3* later in 2013.

Other Titles by Silvia Violet

Finding Release (Wild R Farm 1)
Arresting Love (Wild R Farm 2)
Wolf Caller
His True Nature
Their Natural Habitat in *Cabin for Two: An Anthology*

Available from Changeling Press
Savage Wolf
Sex on the Hoof
Paws on Me
Hoofin' it to the Altar

Available from Silver Publishing
Abandoned (Galactic Betrayal 1)
Deceived (Galactic Betrayal 2)
Needing a Little Christmas
One Kiss

45843414R00109

Made in the USA
Lexington, KY
14 October 2015